INTERNATIONAL PRAISE FOR JAKOB ARJOUNI

"Jakob Arjouni's downbeat detective Kemel Kayankaya has proved as enigmatic as Columbo, as erudite as Marlowe and occasionally, as crazed as Hammett's Continental Op.... Arjouni forges both a gripping caper and a haunting indictment of the madness of nationalism, illuminated by brilliant use of language: magnificent."
—*The Guardian* (England)

"This is sharp, witty writing, packed with life and colour that bursts through in Anthea Bell's translation.... This lively, gripping book sets a high standard for the crime novel as the best of modern literature." —*The Independent* (England)

"Jakob Arjouni writes the best urban thrillers since Raymond Chandler." —*Tempo* (England)

"This is true hardboiled detective fiction, realistic, violent and occasionally funny, with a hero who lives up to the best traditions of the genre." —*The Telegraph* (England)

"A genuine storyteller who beguiles his readers without the need of tricks." — *L'Unita* (Italy)

"A good thriller doesn't need a specific milieu but it can be so much more satisfying when it has one. Jakob Arjouni was born and bred in Frankfurt and does a remarkable job of turning what is often considered Germany's most boring city, into a vivid setting for violent crime capers... This is Arjouni's fourth Kayankaya novel and they deserve to be better known in the English-speaking world.... If you like your investigators tough and sassy, Kayankaya is your guide." —*Sunday Times of London*

HAPPY BIRTHDAY, TURK!

HAPPY BIRTHDAY, TURK!

JAKOB ARJOUNI

A KAYANKAYA THRILLER

Translated from the German by Anselm Hollo

Happy Birthday, Turk!

Originally published in German as *Happy Birthday, Türke!* By Jakob Arjouni

First Melville House Printing: January 2011

Melville House Publishing
145 Plymouth Street
Brooklyn, NY 11201
www.mhpbooks.com

ISBN: 978-1-935554-20-2

Printed in the United States of America

1 2 3 4 5 6 7 8 9 10

Library of Congress Control Number: 2010942260

DAY ONE

I

There was an unbearable buzzing in my ears. My hand struck, time and again, but its aim was off. Ear, nose, mouth—mercilessly it attacked them all. I turned away, turned back again. No way. This was murder.

Finally I opened my eyes and located the damned fly. Fat and black it sat on the white coverlet. I took proper aim, then got up to wash my hands, taking care not to look in the mirror. I went to the kitchen, put some water on, looked for fresh filters. Before long this activity produced a cup of steaming hot coffee. It was August eleventh, nineteen eighty-three. My birthday.

The sun squinted at me, high in the sky. I sipped my coffee, spat grounds onto the kitchen tiles, tried to remember the previous evening. To begin my birthday celebrations in an appropriate fashion, I had splurged on a bottle of Chivas. That was a fact, proven by the empty bottle in front of me on the table. At some point I had trotted off to look for company. After a while I had found the retired fellow who lives with his dachshund on the floor above me and with whom I play the occasional game of backgammon.

I had run into him in the hallway as he was about to take his dog for a pee.

"G'd evening, Herr Maier-Dietrich. How about a little manly conversation over a bottle of firewater?"

He liked the idea, and we made a date.

"Watch out no one steps on your dog by mistake," I called after him, but I don't think he heard me.

I watched a dozen deaths on television and dispatched the first glass of Chivas to my liver. Then Maier-Dietrich rang the doorbell and limped in. He was fond of saying, not without a smile, that the Russkis had stolen his leg.

The evening proceeded according to expectation. We talked about cars we couldn't afford and women we couldn't get into bed. He was past that, anyway. Later we pinched two bottles of Mariacron from the cellar of the greengrocer on the ground floor, and at some still later hour reeled into our beds.

I sipped my coffee, and stared at the empty bottle. Birthday. "Well," I thought, "wouldn't it be nice if someone showed up with a present and a cake." I couldn't imagine who that would be. After last night, Mr. Maier-Dietrich could only be asleep or dead. Besides, he doesn't know how to bake anything, and would probably, forgetful of last night, just present me with a half-empty bottle of Mariacron.

I took an open jar of pickled herring salad out of the refrigerator and poked at it without enthusiasm. The bluish-grey iridescent skin on the bits of fish gleamed in the sunlight. Half a fin stuck out between two bits of cucumber.

I tossed the jar into the garbage, opened a bottle of beer, lit a cigarette. Somewhere a kettle whistled. The sound sliced into my brain.

Then the phone rang. I crawled over and picked it up. "Heinzi, is that you?" the receiver screamed. Heinzi is not my name, nor would I like it to be, but I replied with a cheerful affirmative.

"Heinzi, dear Heinzi, I'm so incredibly glad to hear your voice. I tried to get you all last evening, but you weren't home. Do you know what has happened"

I didn't.

"You know, I went to see the doctor, and what do you think he told me, Heinzi? Heinzi?"

Once more I encouraged her with an expectant "Yes?"

"He told me I'm expecting a baby!"

I began to worry that she might jump out of the phone to wrap her arms around me.

"A baby, Heinzi! Do you understand? At last, at last! It worked—just as we'd almost given up on the whole thing! Heinzi, I'm so happy, and I was right, you see, you just have to really really want it."

I pondered ways of conveying a warning to this Heinzi. "Heinzi, darling, say something? Please?"

"McDonald's fast foods, department of fishburgers and apple turnovers. What can I do for you?"

"What? So it isn't you? Excuse me, I must have dialed wrong."

We hung up. My ears were still humming while I stood in the shower, slowly waking up. The phone rang again, and again. Heinzi must not have given her his real number.

I shaved, dressed, poured the rest of the beer down the drain, and left the apartment.

In my mailbox lay an invitation to purchase pork chops, bathing suits, and toothpaste, and a flier from a mortician. Nothing else.

I scribbled a friendly "Good Morning" on the flier and stuck it in Maier-Dietrich's mailbox. The front door swung open and the greengrocer stumbled in, burdened with bananas. By way of greeting he mumbled something about lazy riffraff and quickly disappeared into his apartment.

I lit a cigarette, stepped out onto the sweaty pavement, and found my green Opel Kadett in a no parking zone a little way down the block. I did have some mail under the windshield wipers. The city was sweltering, and the car almost burned my fingers as I got into it. The air felt and smelled like a sauna someone had left his dirty socks in.

I drove off, enjoying the tepid airstream. It was eleven o'clock, and the streets were empty; people were either vegetating in their offices or lazing by the pool. Only a couple of housewives could be seen trotting down the street with their shopping bags. I squeezed the Kadett into a space two blocks from my office.

My office is in the outskirts of downtown Frankfurt, well protected by a few thousand Americans who had erected their apartment boxes there after the war. Framed by barbed wire, the green and yellow facades go on for kilometres, interrupted here and there by greasy fried-chicken or burger joints.

There is a small bakery just across the street. I went in to get something for breakfast.

Behind the counter stood the owner's corpulent daughter, an impressive advertisement for her father's dough.

She was wearing a garment of daring cut. One could see beige bra straps embedded in pink skin. I waited while an older lady picked out goodies for at least a hundred other older ladies, then purred, "What do you have in the way of tortes today, my dear?" It *was* my birthday.

"Sacher torte, Black Forest torte, rum torte, layer torte, and cream torte." She rattled that off with a smile, then leaned forward and whispered, "But Papa messed up the rum torte."

I decided on two pieces of Sacher, picked a bag of coffee off the shelf, paid, gave her a mysterious wink, and proceeded across the street to number seventy-three.

My office is on the third floor of a medium-sized light brown pile of concrete. Here too I checked the mailbox, with equally disappointing results. The entrance hall and staircase smelled of disinfectant. Quiet whimpers emanated from the dentist's office on the second floor. I slammed the mailbox shut, climbed the stairs, and inserted my key in the office door.

KEMAL KAYANKAYA
PRIVATE INVESTIGATIONS

I became a private investigator three years ago. I became a Turk when I was born. Both my father, Tarik Kayankaya, and my mother, Ülkü Kayankaya, were from Ankara. My mother died when I was born, in 1957. She was twenty-eight. A year later, my father, a locksmith by profession, decided to go to Germany. War and dictatorship had killed off his family; for reasons that remained unknown to me, my mother's relatives did not approve of him, and so he took me along, since he couldn't leave me anywhere else.

He went to Frankfurt and worked for three years for the municipal garbage disposal service, until he was run over by a mail truck. I was put in an orphanage, got lucky, and was adopted after only a few weeks, by the Holzheims. I became a German citizen. The Holzheims had another adopted child, my so-called brother Fritz. At the time Fritz was five, a year older than me. Max Holzheim taught mathematics and athletics at an elementary school, Anneliese Holzheim worked in a nursery school three days a week. They adopted children as a matter of conviction.

Thus I grew up in a thoroughly German milieu, and it was a long time before I began to look for my true parents. At the age of seventeen I travelled to Turkey, but wasn't able to find out any more about my family than I already knew from the orphanage records.

I graduated from high school with average grades, went on to college, dropped out, passed the time with this and that, and applied, three years ago, for a private investigator's license. To my surprise, I received it. There are times when I enjoy my job.

I deposited the torte in the refrigerator and noticed that the interior smelled of mildewed tomato paste. Then I pulled up the blind, opened the window, and kept an eye out for wealthy, good-looking female clients. Heat and light streamed into the office. After putting on water for coffee, I went back to lean on the windowsill. The street remained empty except for a fat, pasty-faced cowboy jogging down the sidewalk. "Congratulations," I thought, and tried to spit into a slipper sitting on a balcony on the floor below me. I stood there staring at those slippers for a while. Then the kettle squealed and I made coffee, scratched dried spaghetti remains off a plate, retrieved the torte from the refrigerator, changed the flypaper, lit a candle, and sat down at my desk. A wasp buzzed in through the window and began to fly in erratic circles, zeroing in on the baked goods. I grabbed a newspaper and folded it and was still in hot pursuit when the door-bell rang.

"It's open," I shouted, and smashed the wasp.

The door opened slowly. Something black slunk in and scrutinized me and my office with apprehensive eyes.

"Good morning," I growled.

The black thing was a small Turkish woman in a mourning veil and thick gold earrings. She wore her hair in a severe braid, and there were shadows under her eyes.

I tossed the newspaper in a corner and said, in a slightly friendlier tone, "Good morning." Pause. "Won't you have a seat?"

She remained silent. Only her eyes darted around the room.

"Ahem..." I searched for things to say. "Is your visit of a private nature, or do you wish to employ me as an investigator?"

"Or as a private investigator," I thought—but even the kindliest audience would not have found that very amusing.

She mumbled something in Turkish, a language I don't understand even when it is spoken loudly and clearly. I explained to her that I was indeed an ethnic compatriot, but that due to special circumstances I neither spoke nor comprehended the Turkish tongue. She frowned, whispered, "Auf Wiedersehen," and turned to leave.

"Come on, wait a minute. We'll manage to communicate somehow, don't you think? Please take the weight off your feet and tell me why you've climbed all the way up here to see me in this heat. OK?"

Her earrings quivered doubtfully.

"I just made some coffee, you see, and . . . well, we can have some coffee and a little cake and—right, that's what we can do. That suit you?"

I was running out of patience. Finally her lips parted and breathed, "All right."

"Make yourself at home. I'll see about a second plate. Just a moment."

Above my office are the quarters of a dubious credit institution whose source of profit lies in the fine print. The clerk of this shop, a sleepy bald fellow, sometimes descends for a chat, usually with a bottle of cherry liqueur under his arm.

Pondering what this mute Turkish woman might want from me, I ran upstairs and banged on the door with the legend: WE MAKE YOUR WISHES COME TRUE—BÄUMLER AND ZANK CREDIT INSTITUTION.

There was a grunt, and I went in. The clerk was sitting behind the reception desk looking bored, turning the pages of a soccer magazine.

"So what's up, Mustafa?"

"I need a plate and a fork. Can you find such things in this dump?"

'What's the dish? Shish kebab?"

"Maybe so."

"I'll see what I can do."

He struggled up out of his chair, lumbered over to a door, and disappeared. There was a sweetish smell in the air.

I walked around the desk and pulled out the top drawer. A half-empty bottle of cherry liqueur rolled towards me. While I unscrewed the cap to take a little hit, things were clattering in the room next door. Muttering curses, the clerk reappeared with a plate and fork.

"Here's your crockery, Mustafa."

He saw the bottle and smirked.

"Still can't get used to the fact that you live in a civilized country, where people don't rummage in other people's desk drawers?"

I set the bottle on the desk.

"Bet you can't get it up anymore. Your wife told me, a while back. Too much booze'll do that, believe me."

He glared at me dully.

"Don't take it so hard, I wasn't so hot myself," I consoled him, took the plate and fork, and left.

The little Turkish woman sat in my client chair, puffing nervously on a cigarette. She gave a start when I entered.

"Sorry, it took a little longer than I thought. Don't you want to take your coat off? It's so hot today."

I served cake and coffee and sat down behind the desk, facing her.

"So let's try this stuff. I hope you like Sachertorte.?"

Her earrings swung a little, back and forth. Maybe that was meant to indicate yes. For a while we ate our torte in silence. Finally she began to tell me her story. I lit a cigarette, leaned back, and listened. She spoke German with an accent and repeated herself from time to time. What it amounted to was this: her husband, Ahmed Hamul, had been knifed in the back a couple of days ago, somewhere near the railroad station. The police working on the case were not—according to Ilter Hamul, Ahmed's wife, who was now sharing my torte—doing their utmost to track down her husband's murderer. She assumed that a dead Turk didn't rate more extensive investigation.

While he was still alive, her husband had given her a considerable sum of money "in case something should happen to me". She did not know where he had obtained this money, but now she wanted to hand it over to me to induce me to find the murderer. She had checked the yellow pages for private investigators, and to her delight she had discovered a Turkish name among all the Müllers. Now she was here. She took a bite of torte and looked at me questioningly.

"I see," I said, wondering what a considerable sum of money was in her book.

"Two hundred marks a day, plus expenses. But I can't promise you anything."

She dug her wallet out of her purse, pulled out a thousand-mark bill and pushed it across the desk. The zeroes looked bright and pretty in the sunlight. "You can give me what's left after you find the murderer."

Her confidence in my skills struck me as a little excessive.

"You live alone?"

"No, I live with my mother, my brother, and my sister. And I have three young children."

"Give me your address, and try to be at home this afternoon, at three o'clock."

"I don't know—my brother goes to work, and..."

"Yes?"

"They didn't want me to..."

"To come to me?"

"Uh-huh, right. They said they thought the police would find the murderer. We should wait and see."

"And why did you decide to come to me anyway?"

"I knew so little about Ahmed these last years. He was gone a lot, and he didn't tell me much. And I had the kids and all that. But I just have to know what really happened—do you understand?"

"How long were you married?"

"Ten years. Ahmed came to Germany in nineteen seventy-one, by himself. His first wife died in an accident back in Turkey. My family has been in Germany since nineteen sixty-five. My father met Ahmed in nineteen seventy-two and brought him home. A year later we were married."

"How old were you and your husband then?"

"I was twenty-six, Ahmed thirty-seven."

"Your father isn't living with you?"

"No. He died three years ago, in an automobile accident."

I took a piece of paper and made notes of some of what she had told me.

"One more thing: tell me when your husband was murdered and where his body was found."

"Friday night."

"And where?"

"In a courtyard, in the rear of an apartment building...near the railroad station."

She lowered her head and stared at the black linoleum.

"You don't know the exact address?"

"No, I don't . . . It was one of *those* houses." The earrings trembled.

Even though her husband had been found dead in a brothel only a short while ago, she had managed to control her emotions quite well until now. I was afraid she was coming close to not managing so well anymore. I got up.

"Good, that's enough for now. Please give me your address, and I'll come and see you at three o'clock."

She gave it to me. We took our leave, and she scurried off.

I lit a cigarette and toyed with the thousand-mark bill for a while. Then I attached it under the desk drawer with a paper clip. Out in the street things had become livelier. The sound of car horns and the occasional shout rose through the open window. I didn't feel too good. "Near the railroad station, of all places," I said to myself. I got up, trotted to the door, and locked it from the outside.

2

It was twenty past one. Lunch hour.

I mingled with the citizens in tight and sweaty shirt sleeves who were streaming out of the buildings in groups of three and four. Depending on rank and status, they were either striding to restaurants or undoing sandwich wrappers and cartons of chocolate milk.

My foot propelled an empty beer can against the back of a flannel-clad leg right in front of me.

"Now wait a minute!" The leg's fat-faced owner stopped and executed a cumbersome turn to face me. "Let me tell you something!"

I gave him a smile.

"Oh, I see! No speaka da lingo, eh?"

He turned to establish eye contact with his three companions. They stood there with big grins on their porcine mugs.

"This Germany! This no Turkey! Here beer cans go in garbage! And Turk fellow drive garbage truck!"

This was accompanied by loud appreciative whinnies. Their potbellies wobbled like jelly. Since I couldn't think of anything to say suitable to the occasion, I left their company and walked over to the nearby garden restaurant, ordered coffee and a Scotch, and thought about Ahmed Hamul and my assignment. I thought about happy hookers, candy-sucking pimps, and good-natured police officials.

Two years earlier I had had some business in the district around the railroad station. A butcher from southern Hesse had wanted to find his eighteen-year-old daughter. He spent a whole hour in my office, shouting and whining until I could well understand his daughter's desire to remove herself from his presence.

I never found out why he had decided to hire a Turkish detective. I looked for the butcher's daughter in all the fleabag hotels, hung out at the station, got punched in the face a couple of times; finally the cops arrested me as a suspected drug dealer. They let me go after twenty-four hours. I called the butcher, told him I was quitting and went to bed for a week.

I ordered another Scotch, another cup of coffee.

Could be some drunken ape had stabbed him in the back just for the hell of it. Or maybe he'd stolen a pair of panties from a whore; maybe he had been running off at the mouth. In the worst-case scenario, Ahmed Hamul had been one of those heroin-dealing Turks that were grist to the mill of the daily papers.

What did I know? All I knew was that there were three round zeroes under my desk.

The neighbouring tabletops were filling up with platters of sauerkraut, bratwurst, and schnitzels. In the muggy air, jaws were tearing into breaded meat, lips smacking, vocal chords groaning and interspersing those noises with occasional speech. Tongues emerged to lick greasy chops.

I had to burp, and a slightly sour-tasting crumb of Sachertorte landed on my tongue. When I began to feel really nauseated, I paid my tab and left.

Ilter Hamul's address indicated that she lived in the district just beyond the railroad station, not a particularly attractive area. I decided to leave my broiler-like Kadett where it was, and set out on foot.

The sun was white-hot above the city, and the bald concrete looked even balder than usual. The stagnant air smelled of exhaust fumes, garbage and dog shit. In the shade of the few sparse trees, retired folks drowsed on benches, waiting for the evening. Children consumed ice cream and ran around on the sidewalks. I trotted through the downtown area, stopping in front of the window displays of several travel agencies to enjoy their pictorial representations of turquoise seas, endless white beaches, palm trees, and smooth brown Bacardi girls. Only two thousand four hundred and ninety-nine marks a week. I considered how many Ahmed Hamuls would have to bite the dust before I could spend seven days building sand-castles, imbibing rum, and having my feet washed by ladies the colour of instant chocolate.

The sidewalk cafés were jammed. Waiters with damp and ruddy faces navigated huge cargoes of cold drinks between the rows of tables.

I approached the railroad station. The sex-shop signs proclaiming "Moist Thighs" and "Sweaty Nymphomaniac Nymphets" did not seem all that enticing.

In this weather, everybody's thighs were moist.

A couple of bums reclined on the sidewalk among empty Coke cans and burger wrappings, wavelets of red wine lapping against the insides of their skulls.

On the other side of the station the streets became empty and silent. I looked for the address until I stood in front of an old building with a crumbling facade. Two Turkish kids were kicking a soccer ball against the wall. I wondered if they'd manage to remove the remaining stucco by evening.

The doorbells had been ripped out, leaving a hole full of tangled wires. I pushed the door open. The hallway was dark. A blend of kids' pee and fried potatoes assailed my nose. From one apartment came faint radio music: I don't love you—you don't love me. Almost all the mail boxes had been pried open or had lost their covers. People had lost their keys. Presumably. Slowly I ascended the stairs to the third floor. At least one member of the Ergün family had been expecting me: as soon as I arrived on the landing the door opened, and Ilter Hamul bade me enter. She had changed her earrings; the ones she was wearing now were small pearls. They seemed much more austere, as befitted the occasion.

Compared to the apartment, the hallway had been a solarium. Vague shapes loomed in the murk.

"My brother came after all. He took the afternoon off," she whispered to me as I stumbled over an insanely placed armchair. We tiptoed down the long corridor as if we'd been about to raid the pantry. The living room was at the far end.

Ilter Hamul grabbed hold of my sleeve, and we entered the large room together.

The Ergün family had assembled there, surrounded by a profusion of colourful quilts, cushions, armchairs, and sofas.

"This is Mr. Kayankaya." She sounded apologetic.

The room was like a glen in the forest. Sunlight streamed through three large windows. Pictures of the homeland hung on the walls. Under different circumstances it would have been quite cozy.

"Good afternoon," I said, trying to sound friendly. One of them nodded.

Ilter Hamul guided me to an armchair large enough to sleep two with room to spare. A teapot, a cup, and a sugar bowl had been placed on a small brass table in front of the chair. I sat down, took a sugar cube, and considered how best to begin. All of them stared at me in silence. The three young children sat close to each other on a red velvet seat. They looked like wax dolls.

"Right," I said, stirring my cup of tea. "As you know, Mrs. Hamul has hired me to find the person who murdered her husband." Silence. Looking pensive, my client's mother cleared her throat. "Or at least, to try to do so," I added. "That means that I have to ask you a couple of questions. It won't take long. Mrs. Hamul has already told me the most important things."

Ilter's brother was sitting to my right, on a dark blue sofa. He cast a quick angry glance at her, but she kept staring at her shoes.

I pulled notepad and pen out of my pocket, found an empty page, turned to Ilter Hamul. "By the way—where is your sister? Is she working?"

Her eyes strayed from her shoes, her lips parted. "Er…"

Her brother replied for her, in a cold, staccato voice.

"She is not well. She is in bed. She can't get up now, she has to sleep."

The atmosphere was about as relaxed as the final minutes of a world soccer championship. All right, stop pussyfooting, I told myself. Let's get this over with as quickly as possible.

"I am, of course, sorry to hear that. Well then, why don't you all give me your names, dates of birth, professions, and so on…"

Since that elicited no response whatsoever, I conjured up a smile and turned to the brother. "Let's start with you, all right? And I would also like to hear your ideas on why your brother-in-law lost his life."

At this point, I was no longer sure what I should ask these people. I didn't expect to learn a whole lot from them.

"My name is Yilmaz Ergün. I am thirty-four years old. I'm a carpenter by trade, but I've been working for quite a while in a cafeteria kitchen. I'm an assistant chef now." There was a trace of pride in his words.

"What cafeteria? Where?"

"At the Hessian Broadcasting Corporation."

Bad radio and bad schnitzels, I thought.

"And what is your opinion about your brother-in-law's death?"

I glanced at Ilter Hamul to make sure that she was all right. She was.

"I don't know anything about it. It's a matter for the police."

I had known his attitude all along. Nothing short of a bottle of raki would loosen his tongue.

"All right, let's leave it at that. Mrs. Ergün, your turn, if you please. The same questions."

The grandma was a little more forthcoming, but it seemed to me she wasn't telling me all she knew. She embroidered her data, digressed into autobiography, even smiled at me once in a while.

She said her name was Melike Ergün. She was fifty-five years old. At the age of eighteen she had married her husband, Vasif Ergün, who had passed away three years ago. They had had three children, Ilter, Yilmaz, and the indisposed Ayse. After they had moved to Germany, she had worked cleaning other people's houses. Recently, she had been looking after her sick daughter.

"May I ask what is wrong with your daughter?"

Before she could say anything, her son spoke for her. "Until about six months ago she too worked as a cleaning woman. Then she lost her job and became depressed." His good German, his apparently secure job situation, and everything else about him seemed to indicate that Yilmaz Ergün was an industrious and conscientious person.

"How old is she?"

"Twenty-four."

"I see. Mrs. Ergün, do you have any ideas about your son-in-law's death?"

I expected her to have a lot to say.

"I think that Ahmed committed suicide."

I gave her a nonplussed look.

"But—he had a knife stuck in his back, didn't he?" I asked Ilter Hamul.

"Doesn't matter. You'll see. He killed himself," Mrs. Ergün said.

I noticed a visible tremor in my client, and decided to change the subject. "All right, I'll raise that point when I talk to the police. Mrs. Ergün, tell me what your deceased husband did for a living? Where did he work?"

Just like my father, Vasif Ergün had taken care of other people's garbage, to his dying day.

"Mrs. Hamul—this morning you told me that you didn't really know, these last couple of years, what your husband did for a living. What exactly did you mean by that? Did he spend a lot of time away from home? Did he travel, stay away overnight?"

I was relieved to see that her brother did not think he had to speak for her too.

"No, no. He came home almost every day," she said, a little hesitantly.

"What did he do? Or wasn't he working?"

"No, he was working."

After Ilter and Yilmaz had exchanged some words and angry glances, it turned out that no one really knew what Ahmed Hamul had been up to for the last two and a half years. Before that he had worked a regular job in a factory, but then he had quit. After that he had told them that he was working as temporary help in the post office, and also in a kebab shop. He had never told them much, but he had always brought home enough money for them to get by. No one knew anything about his friends, or whether he had had any. This was, obviously, a rather taciturn family.

It was equally obvious that my client's mother and brother had not been particularly fond of Ahmed Hamul. I decided to wind up the conversation.

"All right, that'll do. But tell me—would it be possible for me to have a moment with your sister sometime soon?"

All of them opened their mouths, but only the brother spoke. "That won't be possible anytime soon."

Why had I even bothered to ask, I told myself. I stood up.

"OK, I'll take a look around the neighbourhood. I'd like to drop by again sometime tomorrow. Will someone be home?"

"Yes. I'll be here. Because of Ayse."

I turned to Ilter Hamul. "Before I forget—I need a photograph of your late husband."

"Of course."

She went to a desk, opened a drawer, and handed me a large portrait photograph in colour.

Ahmed Hamul had had a thick head of black hair, an equally vigorous moustache, and ears that stuck out, just like any number of his compatriots.

"Thank you."

"Will the police make trouble for us when they find out that my sister has hired an investigator?"

I was beginning to find this brother irritating.

"No, they can't do that. Believe me, they can't." Silence. "Time for me to go."

With greater or lesser degrees of cordiality, all of them said goodbye to me. The children, who had become increasingly restless during the last ten minutes, came alive and started tickling each other. They did not seem particularly concerned about their father's demise. It probably hadn't really dawned on them yet. Ilter Hamul piloted me back through the tunnel. I ran down the stairs and came to a halt outside the front door of the building.

I stood there for a moment, lit a cigarette, and watched the traffic at the beer kiosk across the street.

The interview hadn't been all that exciting. But what else could I have asked those people? Nothing, I told myself. I crossed the street to have a beer. Three hairy creatures leaned about the place, clutching their bottles of Henninger beer. The air had a sour smell. Dim eyes embedded in swollen pink rolls of flesh scrutinized me with sideways glances. One character exploded into a series of hearty burps. Small food particles flew through the air. Between burps, he managed to exclaim, "Hey, I could sure use a Jägermeister!"

"One Pils, please," I called across the vacant counter. I waited.

"I need a Jägermeister! Right, Hans? We all need a Jägermeister!" Silence. "Right?" Clinging to the counter, he turned, slowly and cautiously.

"Right, Hans, we need a Jägermeister! Hans!"

Hans was busy pissing in the gutter. He grunted and passed his hand through the yellow jet as if to make sure that everything was in order.

Finally the door at the back of the kiosk opened, and Madame Hulk trundled in. "A Pils, please," I said, and put two marks in the money tray.

"Why don't you tell me now how many you'll be having? So I won't have to run back and forth all the time." She was a pro.

"OK then, make it two."

"That's more like it."

She heaved herself over to a refrigerator that looked like a pack of cigarettes next to her ample form and managed to extract two bottles.

"Could you open one of them, please," I said, and added the proper amount to the coins on the plate.

The opened bottle landed on the counter so hard the foam flew. Then Madame Hulk trundled back to her den.

I drank my beer and pondered why Ahmed's mother-in-law believed he had killed himself. Then I noticed that the third member of the Jägermeister club was staring at me. He addressed me, with some effort. "You speak good German. You're from the Balkans, right?"

He waved his thumb past his ear, indicating the presumed direction of the Balkans.

"No, man. I just spent two weeks on Majorca."

"Oh, right." A pause. "Nice down there?"

"It's nice, all right. A little dangerous, though, because of the Indians."

"Oh, right." He mulled that one over.

"Were you able to communicate with them?"

"Sure. I used my talking drum," I told him. I finished my beer and walked away without waiting for the next "Oh right."

3

First of all, I wanted to check with the cops to find out what exactly had happened to Ahmed Hamul. I wasn't sure they'd tell me. They probably wouldn't.

It was a bit of a walk to their headquarters, and the second bottle of beer was sticking out of my coat pocket. Since I couldn't very well visit the cop shop with a bottle under my arm, I opened it with the aid of the next metal edge I saw and finished it off. Before I got to my destination, I bought a pack of chewing gum. Then I entered the police headquarters.

The entrance hall was large and painted a light yellow. A long wooden counter stretched across it. Behind that counter I spotted a human head. The head did not turn in my direction, but said, "Can I help you?"

A small, dirty ventilation fan hummed on the ceiling. Its noise blended with some distant trilling sound. I crossed some fifteen metres of floor space, put my elbows on the counter, and said, "Yes, I would like to speak to the detective assigned to the Ahmed Hamul case."

"The small, thin-faced man who had been hunched over a typewriter, papers, stamps, and more papers, looked up. He had a large, red, runny nose.

"Who? Ahmed Samul?"

"No, Ahmed Hamul—the guy who got killed a little while ago, near the railroad station."

"A Turk?"

With a contented expression he inhaled all the snot back into his brain.

"Yes. That too."

"Oh yes, well, you too, right . . ."

"Yes, I'm a Turk as well. Now please be so kind as to tell me to whom I should talk about this matter."

He stuck his finger up his nose and stirred things around a bit. It was almost possible to observe the snot-filled brain at work. Finally he said in a plaintive tone, "Well, I really don't know if I can help you with that. What I mean is, I don't know if it's proper for me to do so. You see, anyone could just walk in off the street, and . . ."

"Listen: I am an envoy from the Turkish Embassy, and I have orders from the highest authority there to interview the detective who is handling this case. If you don't start picking up a little speed, I may have to file a complaint against you."

He looked at me with an incredulous expression and sniffed. Then he became animated. "Oh, in that case . . . of course, naturally . . . It's just that you never know . . . I am sorry. Now if you could just wait a minute, I'll make a call, it won't take long. I hope that the detective in question is in his office.

He rushed over to the telephone.

"Hello, operator? Yes? This is Nöli at reception...Yes, could you tell me who is working on the Ahmed Hamul case? Yes, it's urgent! It's a man from the Embassy! What? What Embassy? The Turkish one, what else! All right, all right—I'll wait."

He gave me an earnest nod.

"Yes, hello, yes...who? Detective Superintendent Futt?... You are in your office...What's the number again? One-seventeen? Very good then, all right, thank you."

He hung up and snorted.

"Superintendent Futt is in his office, on the fourth floor. He's expecting you. Now if you go back into the hall there, you'll find the elevator to your left, about ten metres to your left. Take it up to the fourth and turn right. The fifth or sixth door down the hall should be one—seventeen."

After I had thanked him and he had apologized once more, I left him and took the stairs to have a moment to decide what I should say to Mr. Futt. I had been told that he was a pretty tough guy. I passed more Nöli types laden with files, some unattractive policewomen, and numerous other friends and helpers before ending up in front of door number one-seventeen. I knocked and entered. Futt stood by the window, tanning his bald pate.

"Ah, there you are. You must be the envoy."

A metal desk, two metal chairs, and four metal cabinets adorned the otherwise empty room. The monotony of dirty white walls was relieved only by a calendar with a picture of a jumping German shepherd.

"Good afternoon, Superintendent. Yes, the Turkish Embassy has sent me to find out the facts in the Ahmed

Hamul case." Futt was circa six feet four; his bald head had dents in it, his chin a vertical cleft. He wore a pink shirt unbuttoned down to his navel, and around his neck hung one of those gold chains that look like a prize from an arcade game. He held a cigar between the fingers of one of his strong, hairy hands. The smoke hung in a thin fog in the air between us. He looked like a butcher on vacation.

"Have a seat. I don't really have all that much to tell you. So far, our investigations have not been very productive."

We shook hands. His palm had the texture of low-grade toilet paper. He led me to one of the chairs, sat down at his desk, opened a file, and said in a matter-of-fact tone, "I don't know what details you're interested in, but I can give you all the facts we have come up with so far." He coughed.

"You must have access to Ahmed Hamul's personal data, so we can skip those . . . Last Friday, Hamul was found dead with a knife in his back, in the district around the railroad station. His body lay in an interior courtyard. A woman living in the building discovered it that evening when she was on her way to dump the garbage. Hamul had been living with his wife and his wife's family for ten years—ever since they were married. He worked in a small factory that makes parts for electrical appliances. We questioned every person who lives in that building, but no one knew anything about him."

That was brief. And short on details.

"I regret to say that's all I can tell you at the moment. Please believe me, I wish we had been able to find out more."

All along I'd been wondering why a man in his position was so ready and willing to provide me with information, incomplete as it turned out to be. Had he received directives from above to be accommodating to envoys of the Turkish dictatorship?

What the hell, I thought, why not ask him the things he hasn't told me.

"What is the name of the street, and the number of the building? What is the name of the factory where he worked? When exactly did he die, according to the doctor's report? And do you have any ideas who might have killed him?"

Just as I had expected, he became suspicious.

"Tell me, why do you want to know all those things? I'm sure you understand that we have to keep our information confidential."

"The security services of my government have reason to believe that Ahmed Hamul was the victim of an assault by Leftist radicals, people who have fled the country and gone underground here in Germany. That's all I can tell you. The matter has been classified top secret, and I myself know no more than that."

Bingo.

"Oh well, that puts a different complexion on things, doesn't it? Please forgive me, I was not aware of that. We have been treating the case as a run-of-the-mill murder, if you see what I mean?"

I did. I was beginning to enjoy the game. I produced my pen and notepad and leaned back with a suitably sombre expression. Futt opened another file.

"All right—you have something to write on? Good... the address is Sumpfrainerstrasse twenty-four. The factory is Fuchs & Son, Electrical Parts...You got that? Good. According to the doctor's report, death must have occurred instantly, probably around eighteen hundred hours...As to possible suspects, I regret to say that I have to disappoint you...Frankly, you seem to have made more progress in that respect than we have."

That was enough for me. He probably didn't know much more in any case. I got up, pocketed my pen and notepad and took a stride toward the desk. He got up too, and we shook hands again.

"Superintendent—I really appreciate this. Should we have any further questions, I'll get in touch with you. You have been a great help."

We wished each other a good day, and I left him to his German shepherd. It was six o'clock, time to change shifts, and the hallways were buzzing. Just to the left of the staircase was a switchboard tended by a buxom blonde who clearly had a problem finding the right size uniform. Still enjoying my status as a VIP from the Turkish Embassy, I stopped and gave her a big smile. She scrutinized me with raised eyebrows.

"Hey, Aladdin—where did you leave your lamp?"

At the beginning of my career as a private investigator, I had ordered a stack of business cards, thinking that this was the proper way to go about it. I hardly ever used them, but always carried some on my person. Here was an opportunity. I pulled a little card with the words KEMAL KAYANKAYA, PRIVATE INVESTIGATIONS out of my brief case, slapped it on the blonde's desk, and growled, "Give that to Superintendent Futt when he leaves—or take it to his office. Don't forget, now."

She didn't bat an eyelid. "All right."

Whether it was a wise move or not, I enjoyed the thought of the expression on Futt's face when he saw the card.

I went down the stairs, paid a brief visit to the counter to inform Nöli that he could expect a disciplinary hearing for his earlier behaviour, and stepped out into the sunshine. Rush hour traffic sloshed through the streets. I didn't feel like diving into it, and stopped at the nearest bar. Over a beer I wondered whether I was beginning to behave like a cop. My stomach put an end to that. I decided to go home to the refrigerator, which still contained two or three hamburgers. It was a long walk, and I had time to figure out my further plan of action in the service of Ilter Hamul.

4

TURK!
HANDS OFF AHMED HAMUL!
FIRST AND LAST WARNING!

I held the piece of paper up against the light. No watermark, just ordinary white typing paper. Anything else would have surprised me. Whoever had taped the note to my mailbox had been pretty quick off the mark. The text wasn't particularly inventive. Then again, it probably didn't mean to be.

I took a drawing pin and stuck the note to the wall above the stove. I could study it closely there. Then I unwrapped the waxed paper from the hamburgers, tossed them in the skillet, opened a can of peas, and tossed them in too. The letters had been cut out of newspapers and pasted to the sheet. I had never believed people really did that, and even now I wasn't sure whether I should find it amusing or not. I took my apartment key, ran down stairs and around the corner, and bought all the major dailies. On the way back I glanced at two front pages. The H in HANDS and the I in WARNING came from the same headline. I opened the apartment door and walked into an ambiance of burnt hamburgers. I whipped the skillet off the stove, dumped everything on a plate, opened a bottle of beer, put the papers on the table, chewed, and read.

The headlines of two papers sufficed to provide every single letter of the note. TURK came from the spectacular headline TURK BEATS DACHSHUND TO POINT OF HEART FAILURE. I had spent only six hours with the former Ahmed Hamul. Only the Ergüns, and Futt, and possibly some of his colleagues were aware of this. Did that taciturn family have a talkative member, after all? Or did the police have an aversion to letting anyone moonlight on their turf?

There was one further possibility. What if I had accidentally hit the bull's-eye in my spiel as an envoy from the Turkish Embassy? After he received my business card, Futt must have called the Embassy to make enquiries. What if the Embassy people hadn't just burst into peals of Oriental laughter, but had smelled a rat? Maybe it worried them that some obscure compatriot was spreading information they themselves wanted to pursue. Maybe Ahmed Hamul's death fit into the plans of Turkey's dictators, but they did not want to be associated with it.

One after another, questions came to mind that I would have to ask the Ergüns. Had Ahmed Hamul been politically active? Had he received a lot of mail from the homeland? Had he perhaps joined—here in Germany—a bowling club whose members were seriously committed to the overthrow of the Turkish government?

I picked a crumb of ground meat from between my teeth, took the scissors-and-paste job off the wall, and examined it.

Would the Turkish Embassy use the salutation "Turk"? Well, why not? I lit a cigarette and looked up the Embassy's number in the phone book. I let the phone ring eight times. The receptionist must have gone home for the day. I hung up.

Christmas, Easter, and Whitsun are the holidays before which every German wraps packages to send to his or her relatives. In preparation for this onslaught of mail, the post office hires temporary workers to deal with the mountains of carefully wrapped cookies and pyjamas. The railroad station is the centre of their efforts, and if I wanted to find out something about Ahmed Hamul's life as an occasional labourer, I would have to go there and ask around. I had another beer. Through the wall I could hear a Western movie hero's voice booming out of the set in the apartment next door, whose inhabitant was a shaggy social worker.

I too would have preferred to watch some Indian wars, but I shuffled out again into the light blue August evening.

Birds were twittering in the sleepy rays of the setting sun. It was pleasantly warm.

My Opel was still there in front of the office. I passed it on my way to the nearest subway station. The escalator carried me down into the clammy corridors. Two characters with glittering pink hair and a lot of hardware in their faces reeled towards me. I pulled a ticket out of the machine and sat down on a bench. Next to me three old men were recounting their adventures in the old folks' home.

The train thundered in. The three men carefully got up and tottered to the sliding doors. Tired of listening to clacking dentures, I took a seat at the other end of the car and studied the advertisements.

"Take a Lick!"

The advertising card depicted an oblong plastic cylinder with a tube of vanilla ice cream inside it. For a lick, one could push the tube out, then pull it back again, until the ice cream was all gone. Why hadn't I ever thought of going into the advertising business? How about a can with a shoe brush on top, and when you tickled that, pink raspberry juice would flow...

The train stopped and I dived into the chaos of the railroad station. A youngster waving a bouquet almost ran me down. Two slit-eyed Minoltas wanted to know where women could be obtained. Finally I reached one of the ten post office windows and contemplated the back of an employee.

"Good evening. Hey, could you tell me who to see about a job with the mailbags?"

"Huh?"

"I have a lot of muscle but no work."

"Huh?"

"All right, what I want to know is where I can find the guys who load parcels and packages and such?"

At last, he turned and waved his thumb in the direction of downstairs.

"Track One. There's a door, says Mail."

"Thank you."

"Uh."

I found the door, pushed it open. Another window, another back, another bout of repartee. He pointed me to the nearest door, indicating that the personnel manager could be found somewhere behind it. I entered a hallway and walked past a big cage filled with parcels, then some kind of changing room, and finally came to another door, with the sign PERSONNEL OFFICE. I knocked, but didn't wait for a reply before entering.

"Never heard of waiting to be asked in?" came a grumpy voice from a corner. It was Flabby. Flabby had a red skipper's beard with a clean shaven upper lip, a pimply forehead, and greasy hair combed straight back.

The office was nondescript: cheap pressboard furniture, grey linoleum floor, car dealer's calendar, lighting like that in a public toilet.

The bottle of beer hadn't quite managed to reach its hiding place behind a pile of documents.

"I'm sorry. I knocked several times."

"What do you want?" he rumbled.

"I would like to know if a certain Ahmed Hamul ever worked here, loading parcels."

"Possibly. A lot of people have worked here."

"But I have to know the dates. Surely there's a file on him, if he ever did work here."

"Why do you want to know that?"

I produced my license.

"Well?"

"The guy is dead, and I've been hired to find out what he was up to while he was still walking."

Flabby raised his eyebrows. "All right, I'll have a look-see. When was he supposed to have been employed here?"

"Some time in the last two, three years."

Flabby farted.

"Beg pardon."

He got up and shuffled to a shelf full of files.

"Last two or three years, eh?"

"Yes, that's what I'm told."

He pulled out two folders, tucked them under his arm, and lurched back to his armchair.

"Many of them work here only for a short while . . . Let's see . . . What was his name again?"

"Ahmed Hamul. Spelled just the way it sounds."

"Uh huh . . . You folks all sound the same . . . all right . . . Hamul . . . Ha . . . Ham . . . ," he leafed through the file, "Ha . . . Hamu . . . Hamul! There he is. You're right, he worked here for a couple of weeks at a time, on several occasions."

"When exactly?"

"Here, why don't you see for yourself," he muttered and handed me the file.

Ahmed Hamul, fourteenth April nineteen eighty-one through second July nineteen eighty-one was the first entry.

It was followed by others indicating ever shorter periods, up to the last one, twentieth December nineteen eighty-two through third January nineteen eighty-three.

I closed the greasy folder and asked, "Do you think there's anyone here who remembers him?"

"Possible. Why don't you ask up front? I'm sure someone knows."

"Will do. Have a nice evening."

"You bet."

I left Flabby and went back to the window. Another posterior view. I knocked on the glass pane, and the man turned around.

"It's you again. Did you find the boss?"

"I found the boss. Now, do you happen to remember a temporary worker by the name of Ahmed Hamul? He did several stints here."

"Listen, you better ask the boys out there by the tracks. They would have been the ones that worked with him."

I returned to the booming railroad hall. On Track three, a mail car was being unloaded. I walked over and watched the strong men at work.

One of them took a cigarette break. I walked up to the six foot-six hunk and tried a comradely "Good evening."

"Same to you," he growled. He turned, jumped back into the car, and started heaving mailbags out of it. When he reappeared at the edge of the car I shouted through the noise, "Hey, boss, you happen to know a fellow by the name of Ahmed Hamul?" He disappeared again, returned with more bags, and roared, "Yeah. He worked here for a while."

"Anyone here who knew him at all?"

It took a while before he appeared again.

"Why don't you ask them up there in the shack? They're on break."

He pointed at a corrugated iron roof and was gone before I could shout, "Thank you!" So I didn't.

The door to the place was also made out of corrugated iron, and squeaked most unpleasantly. I walked into a fug of stale beer and cigarette smoke.

Three men sat playing cards at an overturned Henninger crate. A fourth sat in a corner dimly staring at the neck of a bottle. All of them wore greasy sleeveless undershirts that showed off their massive muscles. The card players glanced at me when I entered, but turned back immediately and continued their game of skat.

"Where were we?"

"Seven?"

"Uh-huh."

"Thirty?"

"Shit fuck piss hell! Bet you don't get laid anymore! You're getting so lucky it's illegal!"

"Nah, brains is all it takes."

He reached out for a card, closed his eyes tight. The third one scratched his crotch, looking bored.

"What you got?"

The one with brains tossed two cards back on the table.

"Your girl's best friend!"

"Diamonds, and thirty-three? Gimme a break!"

Seemingly unperturbed by my presence, they started slapping cards on the table. I went and sat down next to the silent drinker, who was still contemplating his bottle.

"Evening."

He turned his head a degree or two, and I saw that his eyes were watering. Among the hairs on his left arm a tattooed mermaid undulated.

"Wha' you want?" he whispered in a tiny voice.

The short attention span of these postal people was beginning to bug me.

"Can you remember a guy whose name was Ahmed Hamul? He used to work with the mailbags around here."

He stared at me a while longer with his wet eyes, then retuned his gaze to the bottle.

"I don' work with foreigners."

Only the sight of his bulging muscles kept me from punching him in the nose. I had had enough. I stood up, walked over to the card players, saved my salutations, and growled, "Listen, you guys, does anyone here know Ahmed Hamul? If so, please raise your hand and shout 'present!' "

They stared at me. I was on a roll.

"For God's sake, is that so hard to answer? A black-haired Turk with a moustache and Dumbo ears—worked here for the last time last Christmas. Just say yes or no—that's all I ask. I don't care if you boycott Black Sea resorts, or if you believe that Turks have rat's tails in their shorts! Is that clear?"

One of the men, the one with the greasy hair combed straight back, slowly put his cards aside and got to his feet.

"Man, I don't know who you are, but I don't like your attitude. You better make tracks while the going is good."

He emphasized his words by slamming the back of his right fist into his left palm. Several times.

With a quick glance at the door I added a little oxygen to my lungs and hissed, "Listen carefully, mailman, no one here wants to know if you like my attitude or not. I haven't lectured you on the uses of soap. All I'm interested in is this: have you ever heard the name Ahmed Hamul?"

I did my best to give him the threatening stare. The other two, amused by my grimace, looked eager for further developments. Suddenly the shack felt very small and quiet. Only the distant hooting of departing trains could be heard through the corrugated iron walls. The monster in front of me looked down at the floor, scratched his chin briefly, advanced three steps, and let me have it.

Small white dots sailed through the dark, jitterbugged, described circles and lines to an accompaniment of uncoordinated church bells. Someone had parked a cargo train on my navel. Probably the guy whose resonant laughter echoed through my skull. From far away came the roar, "Soap, eh? But *he* spews like a sow!"

Cautiously I opened my eyes, and saw a table leg and a puddle right next to my face. Half-digested peas bobbed on its surface. I had a sour taste in my mouth, yet it didn't feel as if he'd demolished my stomach totally. I tried to move. After several attempts, I managed to sit up against the wall and barf some more. Still sitting there, I dug in my pocket for cigarettes and lit one. The nicotine flowed pleasantly into my veins.

The four mammoths stared down at me with expressions approximating pity.

"Not so cocky now, eh? Taught you a lesson." After a pause, "Your Ahmed did work here, but it was some time ago."

I opened my mouth but managed only a kind of rattle.

After two or three further tries I croaked, "Did anyone here know him personally . . . or does anyone know who knew him better?"

"No one here really knew him. Once a girl came by, she was in a state. She screamed and carried on and wanted to know where Ahmed was. I bet she was a whore, but what do I know? It was quite some time ago."

I grabbed a chair, pulled myself to my feet, and staggered out without saying goodbye. Cool air wafted through the station hall. I dragged myself to a bench and took some deep breaths. It took another cigarette to restore me, more or less. It was ten after eight.

I decided to go home and take a shower.

On the way, I bought my stomach a present. A bottle of Scotch.

5

My investigations had gotten off to a flying start. I wiped the last drops of puke out of my ears and made myself a Scotch and soda.

At some time, who knows when, a prostitute had yelled for Ahmed Hamul. That was what I had found out.

I wondered how much physical abuse I would have to endure in exchange for some decent information, and whether I could charge visits to brothels on my expense sheet. Slowly my second Scotch and soda anaesthetised my bruised stomach. If I really had to locate that prostitute in order to find out a little more about Ahmed Hamul, my search could turn out to be interminable. I did not expect the building at Sumpfrainerstrasse twenty-four to yield anything. Futt and his people had already turned it upside down, apparently without results. Besides, I did not believe that Ahmed Hamul had been skewered on his girlfriend's doorstep. I had discarded the theory that his murder had been an accident. I went to my closet to get a fresh pair of socks and my nine-millimeter Parabellum. I hadn't used it much since I'd taken it to a class at a gun club. I pulled it out from its hiding place between my underwear, put on a shoulder holster, and stuck it in. I probably wouldn't need it, but it might earn me a little respect. I put on a sports coat and looked at my bulging armpit in the mirror. Conspicuous as an African in a tanning salon. But maybe this heavy hint of firepower would give me an edge. I fortified myself with a straight shot of Scotch and left the apartment.

For the second time that day, a swaying subway car took me to the main railroad station. Then I took an escalator down to one of those streets dedicated to carnal desire that I would have to scour in my search for that prostitute.

Bright juicy neon and posters depicting two-hundred—pound bosoms, orgiastically grunting women, and glowing pink mountains of buttocks covered the facades of buildings on both sides of the street. In front of the purple plush curtains of various clubs stood men with pale and rancid faces, urging the passing throng to pay a visit to their establishments. Small but powerful loudspeakers transmitted groans resembling those of slaughtered animals, enhanced by lukewarm disco noise, into the street. In groups of three or four, horny farm boys from the surrounding countryside jostled their way down the street, mouths and eyes open wide; retirees peered into flaking entrance halls, licking the drool out of their wrinkles. Married men cast wary glances up and down the street before emerging from the pink swinging doors of a "Love Inn" and hurrying off. I stood there for a while and smoked a cigarette. All around me there were pale and haggard faces, arms with needle marks, emaciated bodies, waiting. I looked at them and tried to figure out what might make a prostitute run into that railroad station yelling her head off.

A pair of glassy eyes approached me, slowly. They stared through me into some indefinite distance.

"Listen, man, could you spare a coin? I'm starving."

I walked twenty metres to a burger joint, bought a box of minced cow, walked back, handed the box to the kid, and watched him tear the cardboard and spill mustard and ketchup on his shirt. I sat down on the curb next to him.

"Bet you know this scene pretty well, eh?"

He turned his bleak face to me.

"You a cop?"

"No, I'm a Turk."

He scrutinized me with skeptical eyes.

"So? The cops don't care, they hire anybody."

"Listen. If I was a cop and wanted to ask you something, I wouldn't treat you to a burger. I'd throw you in the slammer, and it wouldn't take three days before you'd inform on your own grandma."

He giggled.

"Last Friday, someone stabbed and killed a guy. His

name was Ahmed Hamul. Did you hear about it?"

"Uh huh. Maybe."

"I happen to be interested in who did it."

"Guess you are."

"I'm looking for a girl who knew him. Now it could be she's a junkie, just like you, and hangs out here. Maybe you could tell me where to find her."

For a while he went on chewing on a piece of hamburger bun, his mouth open, crumbs falling out of it. I felt queasy and looked away, at faces that were now staring at us.

"Got a smoke?"

I extracted a cigarette from my pack and lit it for him. Greedily he sucked in the tar. His lungs groaned.

"You're OK, man. I'd like to help you find that girl. It's just that there's so many of 'em here. It's not so easy."

"What do you know about this Ahmed Hamul?"

He shook his head, wrinkled his brow significantly and mumbled, "Nothing, man."

I pulled one of my two crisp fifty-mark bills out of my pants pocket, held it up against the light of a streetlamp, made it crackle a little. He could buy a quarter of a gram for that, a good hit.

Suddenly awake, he watched my hands.

"Or, wait... I do know a little bit about him, maybe even more than that..."

He chewed on his lower lip. "But... could you make that twice that amount... maybe?"

I lit a cigarette and sucked on it until the tip was really glowing. Then I started burning little holes in the brown bill. After I had burned off a corner, he slapped my hand.

"All right, man, give me that, it's enough. I'll tell you."

I shoved the charred bill back into my pocket. "Go ahead, tell me."

"Gimme the money first. It's a deal, OK?"

"Oh no it ain't. How do I know you won't just make something up? Let's hear what you have to say. If it sounds useful, I'll give you the money."

"You're an asshole. I knew it. You're an asshole, like all the other assholes in this fucking scene! For a moment there I though you were a buddy, but you're just an asshole!"

He wasn't entirely wrong either. I was afraid he'd burst into tears. I felt like getting up and leaving him. It didn't feel too good to be paying him for his next fix.

"Come on, stop that shit. I don't find my money in the street either."

He mumbled something inaudible. Then, "OK, what the fuck. I really don't know a whole lot about it, but I heard some things. That dead darkie was dealing. I think he was a heavy dealer, in fact, but I couldn't swear to it. He wasn't a street dealer, at least not here. I once met a guy who talked to him once. And when he died, people were saying, like, that's what happens when you try to do sid-edeals, the guys higher up are bound to get you. Something like that. That's pretty much all I know, and I really don't *want* to know a whole lot more. It ain't healthy."

I considered his state of health.

"You don't have a name for the guy who talked to Hamul?"

"No, listen, not even if you gave me a hundred . . ."

"All right," I said. "And you can't really tell me anything about his girl, either?"

"Nah. There's lots of them that are on the needle. If she was a whore, you better ask a few blocks down the street, but they don't care for interviews too much."

I put the singed bill in his hand, got to my feet, and walked on down. There was a lot going on in the quarter. I noticed a bar with a purple neon sign. I'd have to start somewhere. Milly's Sex Bar. The letter A had a restless flicker. Curtains were drawn across the window, but it bore the legend "Fun Till 4 AM."

I pushed the door open and drowned in a sea of purple. Everything, the wallpaper, the tables, the chairs, the bar, the glasses, the carpet, the pictures, the cushions, the lamp shades, even the people were purple. There weren't too many people, though. More than half of them looked like employees. In a couple of the darker corners sat a few sweaty gentlemen with loose neckties, conversing with scantily clad purple ladies. Tinkling, sultry guitar music added to the murky ambiance.

I waded across soft carpets to a table and sat down on a foam-rubber cushion covered in silk. The lady behind the bar had to be Milly. Many years ago she must have been a knockout. Now no amount of paint could cover up the deep wrinkles. Peroxided tresses framed a wobbly double chin. A leopard-skin outfit accentuated the little rolls of fat above her hips, supported her sagging bosom, and made her look like a little old lady down on her luck who had outgrown her fur coat. Nevertheless, you could tell from the way she was issuing orders to the girls that she was the boss.

I sat there leaning against purple velvet and feeling a little out of place. Then came a draft of air, soon followed by a hank of dark permed hair sweeping across my forehead and the sweetish odour of cheap perfume assailing my nostrils. A half-naked Hessian siren sank down next to me and fluttered her professionally attached false eyelashes.

"Ah, my savage sheik, may I join you?" she emoted. Her voice flowed across the table like melted Camembert.

"Sure. What do I have to do to get a Scotch on the rocks?"

"Nothing. Just wait here. I'm your willing slave."

She got up again, with a little twitch of her skinny buttocks, letting her strong stubby fingers slide across my shoulder as sinuously as if they had been long and thin. I doubted that anyone in this establishment had ever heard of Ahmed Hamul, and decided to proceed elsewhere after my drink. A damp hand curled around my neck.

"Here, my savage sheik," she whispered. I removed her hand from my neck and made her sit down.

"Come, come, my savage sheik, what's the rush, we have time, don't we?"

The "savage sheik" number was evidently all her brain could come up with. She gave me a sideways glance, her eyelids half closed. With her index finger she drew slow circles around her navel. Since I could see the stubble where she shaved her belly, the effect was far from arousing. It was time to get down to business.

"Now listen, my ugly duckling, I didn't come here to nibble on your ear or to whisper sweet nothings in it. I'm looking for someone who knows a man by the name of

Ahmed Hamul. God knows why I walked into this purple laundry room, but now I'm here, and I'm asking you: Do you know Ahmed Hamul?"

It took her a moment to figure that out, but when she had managed to do so, she came up with the inevitable, "Cop?" At last her voice had lost its syrupy tones.

"No, I'm not a cop."

I tossed my license on the table. She read it slowly, word for word.

"Happy birthday, Turk!"

She wasn't as dumb as I had thought.

"And many happy returns. So you're just a miserable snooper, eh?"

"A job's a job. You ought to know that."

That was unkind. I didn't care.

"So. Ahmed Hamul. Have you heard that name before?"

She gave me a look that wasn't as sour as I had expected.

"No, I haven't." A pause. "But here's a word to the wise. You better leave now—the boss doesn't like it when guys like you slow things down here. You haven't been all that nice to me, but I don't mind, and that's why I'm telling you this."

"What does the boss have against paying customers?"

"First of all, you're a Turk, and she's not too partial to your kind. And second, if all you want is a drink, there's no profit in it."

"And who is going to bounce me? That grandma in a leopard skin?"

She glanced at the bar, smiled, and whispered in my ear, "She's got a couple of friends hanging out in the back, and they're pretty tough."

I was beginning to take a shine to her, don't ask me why. Suddenly her face no longer looked quite as stupid, and she had abandoned her cheap imitation of a lovelorn harem girl.

"Let me tell you something, darling. You have a lot more seductive charm in your natural state than behind that sleazy Arabian Nights mask." She favoured me with a non-commercial glance that I could feel in my toes.

"Well, I should hope so."

"How about we have another drink?"

She looked at me again, rubbed the side of her nose, and whispered, "Some other time. Now she's really staring at us. I don't want to get into trouble. You better go now."

"All right. Where do I pay for the Scotch?"

"Up there. You pay her."

"OK, darling. Until next time."

"Until next time, my savage sheik," she said under her breath.

I struggled through the carpet to the bar. Milly stood leaning against it, a golden cigarette holder between her shiny red lips.

"How much is the Scotch?"

She scrutinized me grimly. Then she growled, not removing the cigarette holder from her mouth, "Eighteen, sir."

I put my second fifty-mark bill on the bar. While she was making change, I said, in a low voice, "Last Friday a guy was stabbed somewhere around here. Name of Ahmed Hamul. I'm looking for people who knew him."

She gave me a quick glance. "I don't know any Hamuls."

She pushed my change across the counter.

"And I don't like people snooping around my shop. I like them even less when they've got funny bulges in their clothes. I should keep you here and call the cops, but I have a heart, I don't want ten Turkish brats to lose their dad. So. Get out of here."

If it was noticeable in this purple haze, my piece of ordnance had to be more conspicuous than I had thought.

"I have a license to carry a gun, and I'm a licensed private investigator. No need to get all wound up about it. Tell me, is one of your girls on the needle? To sweeten her purple working days?"

At first I was afraid that she would sink her long scarlet finger nails into my cheek, but she simply pushed a small white button next to the beer tap. I hastened to pocket my change and turned to face the door with the PRIVATE sign. Two or three seconds passed before it opened, slowly, and out of it emerged three tank-sized types in pinstripe suits with bulges under their armpits similar to mine. Their eyes surveyed the room. Sedately they advanced to the bar and gathered around me like old friends. The shortest of the three wore a mustard-coloured tie with a pattern of small light-green elephants. He looked down at me, placed his paw on my shoulder and gave it a squeeze. I clenched my teeth.

"Well, sports fan, I hear you find it hard to say adieu?"

He gave me a dirty grin. Three of his teeth glittered with gold.

"There's a lot of nice joints in this town. You don't *have* to spend all your money in one place, do you?"

The three of them together must have outweighed me five to one. I realized that, but couldn't resist the urge to smash their clean-shaven jaws.

"How much does your insurance pay for one of those gold teeth?"

"Why do you ask?"

"Because I'm wondering if I should challenge you to a round."

All three of them laughed.

"OK, strong man, the show is over. The door is over there. It's the door to a healthy life."

Gold Tooth jerked his thumb at the exit. While I was still pondering my next move, the other two grabbed my arms and carried me out into the street. I felt like a child being lifted into a bathtub. One of them growled, "Get a move on, man, or I'll break your fucking Turkish nose." Wide-eyed, I exclaimed, "Oh," and pointed at something. Both of them slewed around and stared at the blank wall.

"What the—?"

I tapped the speaker's shoulder, he turned his head and I drove my fist into his face, breaking his nose with a dry crack. He grunted and hit the sidewalk.

His partner glared at me in disbelief, then collected himself and got ready to beat my brains out. I saw his muscles bunch under the tight jacket as he advanced, cracking his knuckles and moistening his lips. The neon cast shadows on his face, but I could see the whites of his eyes. Once he got his hands on me I wouldn't stand much of a chance.

He stopped and gave me a you're-dead-meat look. I rushed him, then stopped abruptly, ducked, and let his right fist pass over me like a flying chunk of concrete. I jumped, grabbed his arm, threw my weight against it, and twisted it heavenward. The bones in it broke with a loud crack, and he roared with pain. His undamaged left kept swinging blindly, and I managed to duck twice, until he scored a direct hit on my chin.

I staggered backwards on the sidewalk and crashed into a lamp post. My legs gave, and I slid slowly to the ground. My adversary lurched towards me, his right arm flapping like a rag. I sat and waited until he stopped in front of me.

"You little Turkish rat, you'll never do that again!"

I rolled to one side and drove the toe of my shoe into the back of his knee. He hit the ground with a dull thud and lay there like a felled tree. I grabbed his good arm and stretched it across my thigh.

"Take it easy, big boy, or you'll need another cast. I'm telling you!"

He shook, and I had trouble hanging on to his arm. Then he gave up, and I was able to draw a breath. He had to be in a great deal of pain from the broken arm. Then Goliath beneath me began to whimper.

"Stop that noise. If you behave yourself, I'll let you go. But first, a question: Do you know a man called Ahmed Hamul?"

He gritted his teeth, and groaned, "Noo . . . Never heard of him."

I added a little pressure.

"You sure you never heard of him?"

He gave a loud groan and roared, “No, goddamn it, I can’t help it, I never heard of him!”

At that moment, the door opened, and a herd of small light-green elephants eyed me with surprise.

I felt no desire to break any more bones. I let go of the mammoth’s tortured arm and got to my feet. Gold Tooth surveyed the carnage. Then his hand dipped under his coat, but I beat him to the draw.

“Hold it right there! Now raise your hands, both of them, nice and slow. Or I’ll let you have it.”

He made a face and obeyed.

Only now I noticed the sizable audience that had gathered to observe the events from a safe distance. It didn’t seem the right place to wave shooting irons, so I stuck mine back into its holster. My remaining adversary also noticed the crowd and grinned, flashing his gold teeth.

“You should have charged admission. I don’t know how you managed to beat up those two, but it must have been a spectacular performance.”

A distant police siren was coming nearer.

“You better pick up your friends. The cops will be here any minute, and they might ask unpleasant questions.”

He looked at me with amusement.

“Thanks for the advice. Gosh, I hadn’t thought about that. You’ve got a smart little head on your shoulders. But you better take care, someone just might use it for target practice.”

I’d had my fill of tough guys with big mouths. Before I left, I checked the one whose face I had remodelled. His nose was bloody pulp slowly dripping down his cheeks and onto the sidewalk. He was groaning. I grabbed his shoulders and shook them. When he opened his eyes, I growled, "Now remember—visitors from abroad should be treated in a friendly fashion. Next time I'll rip your ears off."

He tried to say something, but only hawked up crimson snot.

I left the battlefield and ambled down the street.

A green police car roared past me, lights flashing, the siren going full blast. I was certain that they would find only Milly there, looking surprised and exclaiming, "But my dear officer, we've had no trouble here at all, believe me!"

I made a beeline for the nearest fast food joint and ordered three paper cups of beer. My chin had suffered considerable damage, and the little mouse behind the counter made a disgusted face.

"Never mind that, sister. It's just greasepaint. I'm with the theatre back there, just taking a break."

She laughed. "Oh, I'm sorry, it looks pretty real. What's the play?"

"Shakespeare's *Romeo and Juliet,* in a modern Oriental—Existentialist production that provides a corrective to traditional European models of interpretation."

She looked serious, nodded. "I see."

After a pause, "And what happens in your production?"

"Romeo meets Ali Baba and trades Juliet for the Forty Thieves."

"Uh-huh, and then?"

"Juliet falls in love with the Forty Thieves, but they want to have children with Romeo, and Ali Baba is left out in the rain. At the end, they all make up, swim down the Nile towards a bright future, and sing 'Soccer Is Our Life'."

She looked at me with round eyes. Then she turned and brought me my beer. After I paid her, she asked, "And what's the bloody chin for?"

"To make the audience *think,* dear."

With that I left her, carried my cups of beer to a table, sat down, and lit a cigarette.

The place was really hopping. Americans in shorts crowded around the small green plastic tables, working hard on their perennial smiles. Out of the jukebox in the corner came Mick Jagger's voice bleating, "You can't always get what you want". I'm not too partial to the bawled maxims of superannuated rock 'n' roll stars.

The beer was beginning to have its gentle effect on my brain. I considered going home and to bed. My search for the prostitute seemed less promising by the minute, and I no longer felt like trading blows with troglodytes.

I decided to try my luck with the streetwalkers. Surely they at least would content themselves with spitting at me.

But first I paid a visit to the men's room. Someone had not been feeling too good. A pool of vomit lay steaming in the corner. My stomach contracted and I had to draw a deep breath so as not to add immediately to that pool. I took a fast leak, checked my face in the mirror, wiped some dried blood off my chin, and left the premises.

Ten to twelve. The sky was now pitch-dark. I walked down a quiet side street past a few timid johnnies who preferred to ask their questions about price and quality in the dark, away from the bright lights. Next to a pizzeria, a white patent leather shoe seemed to grow out of the wall. I headed towards that spot. Next to it, the smell of warm dough rose into the street from a ventilation shaft. It was a good spot. If I had been obliged to stand in the street and wait for clients, I would have picked it too.

Long white legs stretched upward from those high-heeled patent leather shoes. A bright turquoise net body stocking covered her belly and bosom, and her lank blond hair was tied in a braid with a matching turquoise bow.

She let loose before I had said a word to her, "Keep walking, buddy. No fucky-fucky for you. I've got my principles." She waved her arm like a traffic cop.

"Never mind fucky-fucky. I just want to ask you something."

But that didn't interest her at all.

"Fuck off, man, stick it up your ass. Scram."

It seemed highly unlikely that she had ever entertained Ahmed Hamul. Her smooth white arms indicated that she didn't belong to the needle sorority either. I walked on, decided to try two more of the ladies, and hoped that I wouldn't find out anything that might prevent me from going home to bed after that. Regrettably, things didn't turn out that way.

As I approached the next doorway, I was greeted by a short net stocking. "Hi, sweetie, you look lonesome." Her bosom threatened to burst through the black satin and slap me in the face.

"Yeah, guess I am. I'm looking for a girl who used to know a man by the name of Ahmed Hamul. Have you heard that name before?"

She crossed her arms and looked at me with astonishment and disgust. "When did the cops start a Foreign Legion?"

"I'm not a cop. I'm a private investigator."

"I see. Well. Why don't you fuck off, then? I'm working."

I wondered if the remaining thirty-two marks in my pocket might impress her.

"I've got thirty marks. It isn't much, but if you can tell me anything at all about Ahmed Hamul, they're yours."

She chewed her green fingernails and looked at me appraisingly.

"But I don't know your Ahmed. At all."

"He was killed last Friday. Somewhere around here."

"Oh. That guy."

"Yes. That guy."

"Let me see your money. I can't tell you anything before you show it to me."

"And afterwards?"

"We'll see, OK?"

When I didn't respond to that, she burst into a tirade. "God almighty, what a skinflint! What's to lose, for a paltry thirty marks? I make that much with one squeeze of my ass."

She was right. Besides, it wasn't my money. I handed her the three ten-mark notes and she stashed them under her garter with a practised gesture.

"Far as I know, the guy used to hang out at Heini's Fried Chicken. It's a couple of blocks from here. I go there sometimes."

I hadn't expected anything nearly that concrete.

"Why do you think that was the guy whose friend I'm looking for?"

"I ate there Sunday night, and a girlfriend told me someone stuck a knife in the back of the Turk who used to play the pinball machine there."

"Who's the friend?"

"Oh, just someone I know."

"How did she know that?"

A small man wearing a hat approached us with mincing steps, staying close to the wall.

"She must've read it in the paper. And that's all I can tell you. Here comes a customer."

"All right. Have a nice evening."

As I walked away, she called out to say that if I ever came up with a little more dough, she wouldn't mind showing me a good time. I pretended not to have heard that.

I knew Heini's Fried Chicken, if only from the outside. Now I stood in front of it and studied the menu. It was a restaurant with a snack bar, and as I walked in the stink of stale grease hit my nostrils. I sat down at a table by the wall with a good view of the whole establishment. Old paper garlands, leftovers from the carnival, hung below the ceiling. Otherwise the room was a uniform light brown, furnished with a careless array of rustic wooden chairs and tables. A stag's head belled above the bar. There were only a few customers. Tanned pimps in white sports coats were entertaining their present or future employees with tales of high adventure. Here and there, single whores sat nursing a corn schnapps. A burping bum slouched in a corner. Twirling his moustache, a tall thin waiter approached me to enquire what der Herr's wishes were. I told him der Herr would like a cup of coffee and a Scotch, and he dashed off again.

I studied the women. One of the prettier ones sat staring at a shiny chicken leg. The waiter returned, balancing cup and glass on the tray, slid both onto the table with a flourish, and purred, "Would der Herr like something to eat as well?"

He really belonged in the restaurant of the Plaza Hotel, serving lobster legs to conventioneers, not in this greasy schnapps joint.

"No thanks, I've had my dinner."

He smiled and slid away.

I spotted the pinball machine Ahmed Hamul had frequented—if I was right in assuming that my thirty marks had been too measly a sum to exercise the net-stocking lady's powers of invention.

I lit a cigarette and walked over to the machine. Pursued by a hundred superwomen, Flash Gordon zoomed across the glass. I decided to use my remaining two marks to play the machine. I had no idea how I would pay for my coffee and Scotch.

I stuck the coins into the slot, pushed the red button, and turned around. The machine rumbled "Oh, yes." The girl with the plateful of chicken looked up briefly and cast an incredulous glance across the room. I shot the ball into the blinking sea of lights, and watched it carom off rubber and plastic. I let it roll and walked over to the girl with the poor appetite.

"Excuse me—may I join you?"

She looked at me as if I had bad breath. "What for?"

"I have a message for you from Ahmed . . . he's still alive," I whispered.

A shot in the dark—but a bull's-eye. Her mouth opened wide enough to accommodate your average watermelon. I felt like the winner of a lottery jackpot.

"Oh . . . yes . . . please sit down . . ." she stammered, and pulled up a chair for me.

"Who are you? And—and what are you saying?"

I took my time sitting down, feverishly pondering my next move.

"I'm a friend of Ahmed's. He's asked me to give you something."

I looked around. Fortunately, there was no one within earshot.

"I'll explain everything later—not here. Do you know of a more private place to talk?"

"Yes, of course . . . We could go to my place, it isn't far, but . . . Why don't we do that, excuse me, but I'm a little confused . . . you know, it's—"

"No problem," I said. "Let's pay up and go."

I waved to the waiter, asked for the check, and remembered that I had deposited my last two marks in the pinball machine.

"This is embarrassing, but I seem to have left my wallet at home. Can you take care of my coffee and Scotch? I'll pay you back."

"But of course."

While the waiter prepared the check, she began to rummage nervously in her crocodile purse. I was sure the waiter would have liked to ask her if she had enjoyed her food, but he had to restrict himself to staring gloomily at her untouched plate and pretending to be personally chagrined. I was sure he really didn't give a damn. From the look of his emaciated body, he was not too partial to drumsticks dripping with grease. She found her money purse and took out a twenty-mark bill. Her hands were shaking.

"You can add my coffee and Scotch to that."

His expression briefly reflected surprise. He had no doubt classified me as a john, and was amazed to see a prostitute treat one of her clients to coffee and a drink.

While he was making change, I went back to my table, picked up my cigarettes, and knocked back my shot. When I returned to her table, she was just putting the change into her purse. I had found Ahmed Hamul's girlfriend, in record time and without assistance. I was pleased with myself. And that was why I didn't bat an eyelid when I watched her collect fourteen marks in change.

The door of Heini's Fried Chicken closed behind us, and we stood in the street. "I live right here," she said, took two or three steps and pushed a battered door. A flickering fluorescent tube cast a dim light on the entrance hall and staircase. Without a word she started up the stairs, and I followed. There must have been many questions on her mind, and she did not know where and how to begin. That was all right by me. I didn't have any answers.

When we got to the second floor I found out her name. It was hand printed in block letters above the doorbell: HANNA HECHT. Hanna Hecht unlocked the door and switched on the light. We stood on a fluffy white rug in a tiny vestibule. The only other things in the room were a blue telephone and a dim pink Chinese lantern suspended from the ceiling. The place was like an aquarium filled with lukewarm cocoa.

There were two doors. One of them no doubt led to Hanna Hecht's bedroom-come-office. She opened the other one.

These four walls enclosed a small stove, refrigerator, sink, and some cheap furniture, and were decorated with pictures of horses, a pink and beige poster with hearts and dancing children, another with the winsome heads of some pop group. A shelf in a corner was filled with trinkets, horse books, a radio alarm clock. The possessions of a Coke-swilling teenager, rather than those of a junkie prostitute.

"Have a seat. Would you like a drink?"

"I won't say no."

"I have vodka and vermouth."

"A vodka would be nice."

"Over ice?"

"Yes, please."

While she went to the refrigerator to get the ice, I had a chance to take a closer look at her. She was tall and had long legs, encased in blue jeans. If she had put on a little weight she would have had a nice figure. Her face was sallow and haggard from drugs, her blond hair looked thin and artificial. I wondered what kind of relationship she'd enjoyed with Ahmed Hamul.

She put my drink on the table, sat down across from me, lit a long filter-tipped cigarette, and stared at me. She looked anxious.

"Tell me, what—what can you tell me about Ahmed?"

I couldn't think of a white lie. I also didn't know that a white lie would be any use, so I decided to give it to her straight.

"I told you a lie back there. Ahmed is dead."

This time she did not open her mouth. On the contrary, she compressed her lips so tight I was afraid she'd hurt herself. Her fingers crumpled the cigarette and grabbed the edge of the table.

"I am sorry about that. But I didn't know how else to get you to let me ask you a couple of questions. I am a private investigator, and Ahmed Hamul's family has retained me to find his murderer."

Trembling all over, she got up, gave me a frozen glare, then spat, "Get out, you fucker!" I had underestimated the intensity of their relationship. Now, in hindsight, the idea of starting our conversation with a few white lies didn't seem so bad at all. But it was too late for that. Pure hatred flickered in her eyes, and I wouldn't have minded leaving on the spot. Instead, I took a big gulp of vodka and growled, "Enough. I just want to ask you a couple of things. If I had been honest, you wouldn't have given me the time of day. Don't you want them to find his murderer? All I know about Ahmed Hamul, so far, is that he was a dealer and had big floppy ears. That's not very much to go on…"

"I'm telling you, get out of my sight! I don't give a shit about any of that!"

I remembered that I'd told her that Ahmed had asked me to give her something. The notion that I had some drugs for her must have been what had got her so excited—not the news that he'd come back to life.

"Just a couple of questions, and then I'll leave, OK?"

Her face thawed. She even gave me a little smile. "All right, but I have to go to the john first."

She left the room. I couldn't figure her out, but I didn't try too hard. I sipped the cheap vodka and thought about what I wanted to ask her.

I heard the toilet flush, and Hanna Hecht returned a moment later. She was still smiling—but now rather like an imbecile.

"All right. What is it you want to know?"

"First of all: how deep into dealing was Ahmed Hamul?"

"Was he?" She pursed her mouth sarcastically.

"Oh, come on, sister. We don't have that much time."

"We don't?"

She cast a glance over my shoulder, and the nickel dropped, but too late. I turned around slowly and faced the open door with an undoubtedly idiotic expression. In the doorway stood the waiter from Heini's Fried Chicken, twirling his moustache and smirking. A few things began to dawn on me. He had not been surprised to see Hanna Hecht pay my tab; what had surprised him was that I had thought she had to pay for her food. Hence, the large amount of change.

The elegant waiter was Hanna's pimp, and she dined at Heini's for free. And there had to be a bell in the other room that she could use in an emergency.

I felt stupid.

"Quite so. We don't have that much time."

Slowly he put his hand in his pocket and pulled out a black handgun.

"Tell me, Hanna, what's your friend's problem?"

"The asshole's been feeding me a line. Ahmed is dead as a doornail. This guy is a snooper, he works for Ahmed's family. He made me bring him up here so he could ask me some questions. That's it."

Now her face had become a distorted mask. She no longer looked at me, but stared at the floor.

"So he doesn't have any goodies from Ahmed?"

"Shit, no."

"All right. Then we'll escort the young man to the door and urge him not to darken it again until further notice. In a friendly but decisive manner, of course."

He waved his girl in the direction of the door.

"Why does it upset you two so much that I want to ask a couple of questions?"

"Questions, my friend, are always upsetting, and if it is possible to avoid them . . ." his left hand fondled the blackened steel, "then one chooses that option. Besides, I have a personal antipathy to people who deal frivolously with matters concerning the dead."

"I respect your ethical scruples, but . . ."

"Enough of this small talk, my friend. I don't have the time nor the inclination to teach you manners. Now get up slowly and come over here."

I obeyed and walked over to him. Suddenly he rammed his gun into my stomach, pushed his hand under my coat, and extracted my Parabellum. Then he shoved me up against the wall.

"I beg your pardon. Just a precaution. So you won't get any silly ideas later and think you can just come back again." He pulled the magazine out, dropped it on the floor, and tossed the gun back to me.

"All right, my friend. Now we'll walk quietly through that door and down the stairs."

Behind me, I heard Hanna Hecht banging the ice tray again, fixing herself a drink. Then I let the polite waiter escort me down the stairs and into the street.

He gave me a few more warnings about things that might be detrimental to my health, took his leave with aplomb, and disappeared into Heini's Fried Chicken.

It was just past midnight. My birthday was over, and it was bedtime.

As I left the subway station, the vodka began to throb unpleasantly in my neocortex. I wandered through the quiet streets and admired the delicate curve of the sickle moon.

When I reached my building, I walked into the driveway entrance to the courtyard and took out my keys. While I was still wondering who the idiot was who had parked his car right in the middle of the drive, its engine revved up and its lights came on and blinded me. The tyres squealed, and I turned and ran the fifteen metres back to the street. Not a second too soon, I managed to slide to the right and under a parked car. A small Fiat shot past me, braked quickly, then thundered to the left. I rolled and turned as fast as I could, tore my cannon out of the holster, and aimed at the tyres.

All I heard was a quiet metallic click. I saw the Fiat disappear around the corner. A window was flung open in the building across the street.

"For Chrissakes, stop that racket or I'll call the cops!"

The window closed again with a crash.

I got up and slapped dirt off my pants. There was a smell of burned rubber in the air. It would have been tempting to go back and pistol whip the waiter with my empty gun, but I put it back in the holster, went to my apartment, and fell into bed.

DAY TWO

I

Madame Hulk looked at me across the counter with puffy, sleepy eyes.

"I'm sorry, but I don't serve coffee. There's no call for it. All my customers ever want is beer, even this early in the morning. It's really a shame. But—listen, I just made a pot for myself. I'll let you have a cup of that."

Without waiting for a response, she shuffled off.

It was nine in the morning. My head was throbbing. I had hit the shower at eight and decided to start the day with a visit to Mrs. Ergün. Now I leaned against the kiosk counter across the street from her apartment, hoping to have a cup of coffee before I went over there.

I had called the Turkish Embassy, but even though I had impersonated an official of the German Department of the Interior, going so far as to affect a Bavarian accent, the gentleman at the other end of the line could not or did not want to tell me anything about Ahmed Hamul.

Coughing and wheezing, Madame Hulk returned with a paper cup of coffee.

"You wouldn't happen to have an open-face sandwich or anything like that?"

"I can heat up some beef sausage for you, if you like."

My stomach signalled: no beef sausage for breakfast, please. I decided to have a bar of chocolate and a pack of cigarettes.

"Will that be all then?"

"Yes."

"My coffee's getting cold."

I watched her mighty backside squeeze through the door and gradually disappear. Her coffee was of that strength they say can raise the dead. I ate half of the chocolate bar, lit a cigarette, and thought about the Fiat with the squealing tyres. I doubted that it had really been the driver's intention to hit me—there were easier ways to get rid of me. It seemed more like an action intended to give a little more emphasis to the hands-off note. And it had certainly been effective.

But who on earth considered me such a serious nuisance? The Turkish Embassy bureaucrats would hardly employ such mob tactics, waiting in the car for hours just to give me a powerful scare.

Or maybe they would?

To gain some clarity on that, I simply had to find out if Ahmed Hamul had ever engaged in political activities. I finished my coffee and walked over to the house with the ripped out doorbells.

Mama Ergün opened the door. She was wearing a green-and-brown-striped terrycloth bathrobe. Her spongy yellowish feet were hard, and her toe nails were the colour of pus. She was as surprised as I had expected, apologized for her informal attitude and asked me to step inside, although she seemed reluctant.

The apartment smelled of toasted breakfast rolls, and I could hear a shower running somewhere. She took me to the kitchen. Two clean plates sat on the table, ready for breakfast, with a basket of fresh rolls.

"Yilmaz has already gone to work, and Ilter is out making arrangements for the funeral. I was just about to have breakfast with Ayse. Would you care for some coffee?"

She didn't have to ask me twice. I kept hoping she'd also offer me one of those delicious warm rolls. I wished I could make my stomach growl at will, not to seem too obvious about it. Instead, I asked her, "Would this be a good time for me to have a word with your daughter Ayse?"

Yilmaz Ergün had made it very clear to me that I was not to have a word with his sister, but he wasn't here now, and I had also noticed that the rest of the family did not entirely agree with his pronouncements.

Even so, my question was obviously putting Mrs Ergün in a quandary. Her words positively dragged themselves off her lips.

"Yes . . . When she is ready . . . you may speak to her."

I began to be convinced that poor Ayse was a victim of syphilis. Her mother poured me a cup of coffee and sat down across the table from me.

"Since I talked to you yesterday, I've been thinking of a whole bunch of further questions, and that's why I'm here so early. To be quite frank with you, I haven't been able to find out a whole lot about your son in-law. All I have to go on at the present moment are certain assumptions. But perhaps you could help me."

I was finding it hard to tear my yearning gaze away from those fragrant golden rolls. She must have noticed, because she said, as soon as I had stopped talking, "Please help yourself, if you like."

Pretending to be a polite person, I said, "No, no, I don't want to eat your breakfast."

"Please help yourself. We have plenty."

"Well, then I'll have one."

I cut the crisp roll in half, slathered butter and marmalade on it, and tried to chew it sedately. Slowly, it coated my stomach with a pleasant warmth.

"First of all, I would like to know a few things about Ahmed's past. I'd like to know if he was politically active in any direction, if he was a member of any party or other organization. If so I would have to know the details about what he did in such a context."

She seemed quite surprised.

"But Ahmed never had anything to do with politics."

Only then did I realize how much unfounded hope I had put on that assumption. It was just like having sat all evening in a tavern engaged in the construction of a carefully planned house of beer mats: at the very moment you are about to put the last mat in place, some fat idiot stumbles and bangs into the table with mumbled apologies, You sit there in front of the collapsed project and feel like breaking the stupid bastard's jaw.

"I see. Well, I didn't really think he did."

It's bad PR for a PI to admit that his analytical abilities are more or less underdeveloped. So now all I had to go on was Ahmed the Dealer.

"You told me yesterday that Ahmed's life became rather disorganized about two years ago. Can you remember any particular incident from that time? Like an unexpected visit or an unusual amount of mail from Turkey?"

She sipped her coffee and remained silent.

"Mrs. Ergün—did you know that your son-in-law was a heroin dealer?"

She nodded, still silent. It was quiet in the kitchen. The first rays of the sun crept through the window and cast deep shadows on her face. She gulped down the rest of her coffee.

"Of course. I knew it all along. Everybody knew. Ilter was the only one who went on believing Ahmed's lies..."

She followed that up with a couple of maxims on the blindness of women in love. Then she came back to Ahmed and to her late husband, Vasif. Just like Ahmed, the latter had come home one day with a lot more money than he could have earned at his low-paying job. About a year before his fatal accident, Vasif had started spending his nights in bars and clubs. Mrs. Ergün knew this because she had tailed him several times on these excursions. He had never admitted it, but everything pointed to the fact that he had been dealing heroin. She had not been able to find out who supplied him with the stuff. There had been no new visitors, no unusual mail. At some time during this period, Ahmed must have been introduced to the same business by his father-in-law. According to Mrs. Ergün, it had not seemed strange that Ahmed and Vasif went out and spent time together.

They had been best friends even before that time. Ahmed Hamul must have seemed like an adventurous soul in that otherwise rather cautious and provident family. The old man had liked him, and besides, Ahmed was only ten years younger than Vasif.

Soon Vasif preferred Ahmed's company to that of his own children, especially that of his son Yilmaz. Vasif and Ahmed's relationship was like that of two happy vagabonds who enjoy plotting pranks together, not the usual relationship of in-laws. This created tensions in the family. Yilmaz, especially, often gave vent to his jealousy by coming up with mean accusations against his father and brother-in-law.

I began to understand Yilmaz's negative attitude towards me. After Vasif's death, Ahmed had gone on dealing by himself and had not put in many appearances here at home. Everybody except his wife Ilter had felt quite relieved. Mrs. Ergün paused, and I observed myself spreading things on yet another roll. She wrinkled her dark, leathery brow and sat there, brooding. Only the squeak of my knife against the china cut the contemplative silence.

I was beginning to get a picture of the Ergün family. There was Vasif, the paterfamilias who had first provided for the family by working as a garbage collector and did not find much joy in this strange land among its sullen, staid inhabitants. His relationships with his children were tenuous. They had been very young when they came to Germany, and had grown up in the new environment. Having no choice, they had adjusted to it, and in the process had grown remote from their father. On the other hand, Yilmaz, a hard and ambitious worker, did not receive much positive reinforcement from a father who would have preferred a livelier son. Yilmaz grew embittered, concentrated on professional success, and probably related only to his mother—to Melike Ergün, the nurturing mother, who had not been strong enough to prevent her husband's transformation into a heroin dealer. But she took care of the children and was the backbone of the family.

Then there was Ilter, shyer and more reserved, the oldest daughter, who helped her mother, soon became a mother herself, and also dedicated her life to childcare and housekeeping. Ayse Ergün was the only one I was still unable to describe. For some reason, she had to be the blackest sheep of the family.

Then Ahmed Hamul, relatively fresh from the old homeland, burst into the sombre family scene. He married Ilter, made friends with her father, and caused a split in the family. On one side stood Yilmaz, Ayse, and their mother; on the other, Vasif and himself. Ilter and the young ones occupied some kind of no-man's-land in between. I looked at a large aerial view of Istanbul that hung framed on the yellow kitchen wall. I asked Melike, "Don't you remember anything out of the ordinary from the time when your husband first became a heroin dealer? Please try to remember! Anything at all. Things that may not have seemed to have anything to do with that."

"No. I don't. Really, I can't think of anything."

"So you don't really know when he started dealing?"

She looked pensive, rubbed her hands together.

"I think it was quite soon after the accident . . . Yes, that's when it started."

"What accident was that?"

"Oh, it wasn't a bad one. Vasif just ran into another fellow's car."

"Did your husband have many accidents like that?"

I bit my tongue. I hadn't meant to ask her that.

"No, it was the only one he ever had. Except for the one that killed him."

It was a very skinny little straw, but it was one to grasp.

"Were you there when it happened?"

"Yes. We were on our way to visit some friends."

"Do you remember the date?"

"No, not exactly. It was in February, but I can't remember the date."

"Whose fault was it? Your husband's or the other driver's?"

"I don't really understand those things, but I thought it was Vasif's fault. The other car came from the right. But then it turned out it wasn't his fault after all."

"What do you mean, it turned out—?"

"Well, you see, the police came, and all of us had to go to the station, and Vasif had a long talk with the police. I wasn't there, I had to wait in the reception room. Then Vasif came back and told me that everything was all right."

"He didn't have to pay a fine?"

"No, thank God, we had very little money back then, and Vasif was quite desperate when they took us in. But then he was happy again, and he didn't have to pay anything."

"The other driver—can you remember his name?"

"No, I can't."

"What kind of a person was he?"

"He was a young man. With blond hair."

There were millions of those. However, the police had to have a record of the accident.

"Do you remember the precinct they took you to?"

"Yes, it's not far from here, three blocks over. The accident happened just around the corner. I can show you the spot from this window."

We got up and stood next to each other by the kitchen window. She described the accident again, in detail. Even from here, it was easy to see that it had indeed been Vasif's fault. We stood there for a moment watching the noisy traffic until I asked her, "Where was your husband going on the day of his fatal accident?"

"It was a Saturday, and we were having breakfast when the phone rang and Vasif had a few words with whoever it was. Then he told us he had to go for a short drive, and that he would he back soon."

She fell silent and compressed her lips.

"Do you remember that date?"

"The twenty-fifth of April, nineteen-eighty." "You don't know who called him?"

"No. It was one of Vasif's friends."

"Where did the accident happen?"

"On the road to Kronberg."

There had to be a record of that too. I decided to leave Mrs. Ergün alone and go to the police. My first question would be directed to the Narcotics Squad. I wanted to know if Vasif and Ahmed had a record with them.

"Mrs. Ergün, you have been a great help. I'll come by again tomorrow, and I hope I'll know more about it then. Could you tell your daughter Ilter to call me today, either at the office or at home? She has the number."

We said goodbye, and I thanked her for breakfast. As I was about to leave, the old woman gave a start, as if someone had kicked her. Reluctantly, her gaze strayed past my shoulder.

The kitchen door opened with a quiet squeak. Cheap scent wafted through the room. I turned slowly and looked in the direction of that perfume. Ayse Ergün stood in the doorway, on shaky pins. Mother and daughter stared at each other in silence. At last I understood.

Ayse's eyes looked like the eyes of someone struggling through a fog. Unfocused, their gaze slid across the kitchen. A light but steady tremor ran through her small, thin body, and her fingers curled into her palms as if she were trying to hide them. Ayse Ergün was not a victim of syphilis. She was on the needle.

2

"Come again—what is it you want?"

He sounded like an ambitious officer dressing down some hapless private for his insufficiently creased pants. His teeth bit off every word so cleanly I was afraid he might do damage to his tongue. His steel-blue eyes flashed at me with irritable condescension. At least he did not pick his nose constantly, like Mr. Nöli.

But for the second time I had to engage in verbal combat with a hero of the reception desk at police headquarters.

"You got shit in your ears? I'm looking for the *Narcotics Squad!* Do I have to spell it out for you?"

He snapped his jaws and squinted as if I had poured boiling water on his socks.

"Don't you dare speak to me like that! I can have you thrown out in the street!" He raised a ruler in a threatening gesture and slammed it on the desktop. The cords in his clean-shaven neck grew taut.

"Don't tell me how to speak. Your kind doesn't understand anything short of a kick in the pants before you condescend to give a halfway decent answer to a simple question. All right, I can find it by myself."

While I was still telling him that, he got up, his face cheesy white. I turned on my heel and left the room. I didn't hear him say anything else. He was probably on the phone, giving orders for my summary execution.

A pair of flesh-coloured nylons frisked towards me in the grey hallway.

"Excuse me, could you tell me where the Narcotics Squad's offices are?"

She scrutinized me with a certain degree of awe. Maybe she thought I was a heroin lord who was finally turning himself in. Maybe she was just fascinated by my chin, which was still adorned with a dark scab.

"They're on the fourth floor."

"Thank you."

This time I took the elevator. Number four lit up, and the scratched doors opened.

First I smelled him, or rather, his cigar. A moment later I saw him. Futt the Butcher stood waiting by the elevator door. Next to him stood a youth of slender build who stopped whatever he had been saying in mid-sentence when his eyes lit on me. I couldn't help laughing.

A fat red vein swelled up on Futt's bald pate, and his fat chest heaved. But the roar did not come. Instead, he broke into a smile like a torturer's assistant who is delighted to see his next victim.

"Ah, it's the envoy."

He sounded beery and cheery, ready to offer me a cigar. Only his eyes narrowed. He could have had a career as a character actor in children's movies—the sweet uncle next door who is fond of making peepee with the little girls.

"Ah, it's the detective superintendent. How is the Hamul case? Are international complications in the offing, or was he just your average darkie? My interest is of a private nature, as you must have discovered in the meantime."

Slowly Uncle Futt returned his cigar to its place between his polished teeth. He inhaled deeply, then puffed out a series of cute little smoke rings. The kid next to him must have heard about me. He was pawing the floor with his hind legs, and I had the impression that he was just waiting for a hint from his boss to hurl himself at me. With his physical proportions, he would probably have to resort to pulling my hair.

Futt blew the last puff of smoke out of his lungs and into my face and said, in the compassionate tone of a defense attorney who informs his client of the execution date, "My dear Mr. Kayankaya—as far as I know, I don't have any urgent appointments this afternoon. Therefore I'll spend some time finding out how to divest you of your private investigator's license as quickly as possible. I'm sure it will be child's play for a man of your talents to find some other form of employment."

"Like, sanitation engineer?" the kid burbled, and twisted his lips into an uncertain smile.

Futt, however, didn't seem to think that was very funny. He gave the kid a look of cutting reprimand.

The pair provided an excellent demonstration of the simply structured existence of master and dog.

Futt raised his eyebrows and continued, "Now, Mr. Kayankaya, I'm not a heartless person, but there are certain things that get my goat. First and foremost, it annoys me when someone thinks he can have fun at my expense. I consider honesty to be one of the noblest virtues, and if you had been candid with me, who knows, we might be working together at this point. Now, however . . ."

He waved his hand in an eloquent gesture. Dog-boy slobbered on his pants leg and gazed expectantly at his master. But Master did not return that gaze.

Instead of barking, Dog-boy spoke up. "Ahem, Superintendent, maybe we should, uh . . . shouldn't we . . . now that—"

Futt's short and decisive "No" struck him like a whip.

I was tired of watching this training session. I asked Futt, "I can tell that he can sit up and beg—but can he retrieve the little stick?"

Futt laughed. Not wholeheartedly, but loudly enough to make me feel sorry for the kid. The kid was looking at me as if I had been spreading rumours about his tiny penis.

"When you're done laughing, you might wipe the snot off your chin, or someone else might have fun at your expense."

He grabbed his chin. I laughed and left him there. Before I found the door to the Narcotics office and knocked on it, I could hear the elevator doors open and the duo getting into it. During that strange game played by master and dog, I had somehow felt as if I were the bone.

A deep voice bellowed a drawn-out "Yes" and I turned the doorknob. The office faced east, and I squinted as I walked in.

It was a large room with three worn wooden desks, one of them hopelessly cluttered with files. It was the one at which the owner of the deep voice sat. He had the face of an intellectual afflicted by migraines. Two large red bumps, no doubt caused by his spectacles, adorned the bridge of his nose. He had taken them off and was chewing on one of the earpieces with a suffering expression. A steaming cup of black coffee sat on the desk. In a corner, a radio whispered weather reports. There was a whiff of fat cigar in the air. So Futt too must have made some progress. The man arranged his face in the grave wrinkles of one carrying a heavy burden and looked at me as if I were his dentist.

Since he did not give any indication that he wanted to speak first, I opened the conversation.

"Good morning. My name is Kemal Kayankaya. Last Christmas I received a private investigator's license. Now, after 'outing' Santa Claus, I intend to prove that that longhair who called himself the son of God was in fact the most notorious hash-smoking hippie in all Jerusalem."

He did not bat an eyelid, but went on staring at me with those migraine eyes. A kind person would have handed him a bottle of aspirin. I was not a kind person.

"May I suggest a method whereby you may avoid the pain of speech? If you wiggle your left ear, that means yes, if you wiggle your right ear, that means no, and I'm only allowed three direct questions. Is that a deal?"

Instead of wiggling his right ear, he said, "No." A brief pause followed, and I wondered if that would be all I'd hear him say.

"I don't know who you are. Besides, I'm not particularly interested in knowing who you are. If you just wanted to drop in to present this comedy routine, I must now ask you to leave. I am a busy man."

He pulled a crumpled handkerchief out of his pocket and started wiping his glasses.

"I came here to find out if the Narcotics Squad has a file on a certain Ahmed Hamul. Last week he ran into a knife, in the district around the railroad station."

He put his glasses back on. Now he looked like a graduate student of German language and literature after a hard night of studying. He was simply out of place in this environment.

"Even if there were a file, you would be one of the multitudes who would never get to see it. Don't waste your time, and mine. Go make your wisecracks somewhere else. If you keep on trying, I'm sure you'll run into somebody who thinks they are amusing."

At the end of his little speech, he folded his hands. He looked exactly like a professor after a lengthy lecture who is hoping that the students won't have any further questions and will now leave quietly.

"Who or what do you have to be in order to see those files?"

"Everything you are not."

"All right, that's that, then. But we'll meet again," I added, without the slightest idea why. While I was leaving the room, the radio oozed something about seven bridges I would have to cross.

I left the stuffy halls of the police headquarters and walked out into the sunny street. A really packed pair of jeans squeezed past me, and I kept my eye on them until a pair of sloppy overalls intervened. I headed for the nearest pay phone to make a call to a retired detective superintendent I know. Theobald Löff had been enjoying his pension for two years. I had first met him when he was looking for a former female client of mine in a murder case. He was the first and only cop I'd met with whom I had found it possible to communicate.

As a man who had retired from the police force with honours, Löff would be able to gain access to the files I needed. I put my two ten-pfennig coins in the slot and dialed Löff's number. The phone rang three or four times. Then a harassed voice shouted to please wait a minute, the milk was boiling over. It was Mrs. Löff. They had been married for some forty years and their union was of the kind described as happy and boring. I stood in the stuffy telephone booth and felt drops of sweat trickle from my armpits, one by one. The booth smelled like digested garlic.

Finally Mrs. Löff returned to the phone and wanted to know who it was. I told her who it was and what he wanted. She said her husband had gone out but would return soon, and why didn't I drop in for lunch? I thanked her for the invitation, slammed the receiver back on its hook, and fled outside.

3

The Löffs live in Nieder-Eschbach, a suburb of terraced houses on the fringe of our metropolis. The numbers on the glass or plastic lights hanging in front of the houses are the only thing that distinguishes one beige shoebox from another. In front of each one lies a manicured little lawn, four by four metres, bordered by carefully planted flowering shrubs, and these in turn are surrounded by a low picket fence, stained brown, whose sharp points serve no other purpose than to puncture the eyes of small children who may fall on them. The air of long summer evenings reeks of charcoal grill smoke, and one can see excited heads of households running about in their dark blue sweatsuits, swinging sausages and pork chops. I steered the Opel down the quiet street at a sedate pace, looking for number thirty-four. Then I spotted it on a wrought-iron coach lamp next to a door of blue corrugated glass. I parked and got out of the car. The only traffic noise was the distant buzz of a moped. Smells of half-cooked food wafted from open windows. Behind a barred basement window, a woman's voice warbled, "Die Gedanken sind frei . . ."

I opened the gate, stumbled over a stupidly grinning garden gnome, and pushed the doorbell button. It responded with a high-pitched two-note chime. Mrs. Löff came to the door wearing a bright floral apron.

"Mr. Kayankaya! Come in, this way. Lunch will be ready in a minute. My husband's in the living room."

For a sixty-year-old, she was in fine shape. Her husband, however, was somewhat at a loss what to do with his free time once he was done tending his vegetable garden. Theobald Löff's favourite pastime consists of regaling willing audiences with stories of heroic deeds from his law enforcement career.

I walked through the low-ceilinged light brown vestibule into the living room. When the Löffs had moved in, years ago, they had first placed a gigantic television set in the corner and then arranged the rest of the furniture around it. A living room suite upholstered in coffee-coloured corduroy faced the monstrous TV, and so did the other easy chairs in the room. Even the lamps were positioned to provide a pleasantly muted background light. On the walls were engravings of various castles and afghans with rustic motifs. Mrs. Löff must spend her long winter evenings crocheting these—at least, that was what they looked like. On two coffee tables lay seed catalogues and television magazines.

Löff sat in his easy chair, hands folded on his lap. He was looking out onto a patch of his garden. When I entered, he got up and shuffled over in his terrycloth slippers.

"Hello, Mr. Kayankaya! How nice to see you again."

I shook his small, thin hand. Löff has an abundant head of grey hair: at first sight, it looks like a fur hat on the slightly built and now somewhat rickety fellow. His face is narrow and covered with little wrinkles like a dried-up apple. His imposing aquiline nose is its most noticeable feature.

"Hello, Mr. Löff, how are you? How is your lettuce doing?"

He made a face, enhancing the dried-apple effect. "Lettuce! That stuff's only fit for children and octogenarians. I tore it all out and tossed it on the compost heap. Couldn't stand the sight of it any longer. What's the point? You spend half the year planting and nursing it, then you have to eat it the rest of the year. My wife wanted to freeze it! That's impossible, I told her. No, it's not, she said. The very thought—to have to chew on defrosted lettuce, every goddamn day! I just tore it all out."

He contemplated his slippers defiantly.

"But enough about that. Have a seat. Tell me why you've come to see me. I'm sure it's not just to enjoy my old lady's lunch sausage."

We seated ourselves on the brown couch. He crossed his arms across his chest and looked at me expectantly.

"No, I didn't come just for the sausages. I'd like to ask you if you think it might add a little variety to your days if you put on your policeman's hat again, and helped me out."

He cast an impatient glance at the ceiling.

"You know very well how I feel about that. Cut to the chase."

I told him my story from the very beginning. I told him about Ilter Hamul's visit, the threatening note, Ahmed Hamul's dealing, the fast little Fiat, Hanna Hecht, Mrs. Ergün's story, Papa Ergün and his accidents—all the way up to my visit to the Narcotics Squad that morning.

Löff listened attentively. I noticed that he seemed to be feeling better already.

"And I think that's the whole story so far," I concluded, and sat back to wait for his questions.

He slipped back into his detective superintendent mode. He scratched his head, got up slowly, found his pipe and tobacco, packed the pipe, and arranged his little wrinkles into a solid frown. I don't think I could have done him a greater favour.

Sherlock Löff lit his pipe and let the smoke trickle through his nostrils with an air of deliberation. "Who is working on the case?"

"Oh, I forgot to tell you. It's that guy who looks like a butcher, Futt, and some tiny character who flutters around his ankles."

"That's Harry Eiler. Futt's shadow, even back when he was still working for the Narcotics Squad. He's really just a cop on the beat, that's all he's good for. Nevertheless, Futt keeps using him as a partner or assistant—I can't see why. He must have his reasons. Futt may be a nasty piece of work, but he's a good policeman."

"'But'? I've always thought those two go together..."

Before Löff could respond to that, his wife appeared and declared in dulcet tones that the sausages were waiting.

The Löffs' dining room looks like the showroom of a plastics factory, a space designed for messy little kids. The pale yellow walls are adorned with recipes encased in plastic. The chairs and the dining table are bright orange, and the floor is covered with dark green linoleum. Our placemats were washable plastic. All it needed was an open drain, and the place could have been cleaned with the garden hose.

Mrs. Löff shoveled sausages, mashed potatoes and sauerkraut onto my plate. I twisted the tops off two bottles of beer.

There were a great many half-raw chunks in the homemade mashed potatoes. But they *were* homemade.

"You can really tell this isn't that instant stuff."

Mrs. Löff thanked me for the compliment.

After we had chatted about the weather, the prices of things, and special offers, and had had a few good laughs at the expense of our new Chancellor, Löff asked me, "Now that I've heard your story, tell me how I am supposed to help you out."

"Oh, Theo, can't that wait until we've finished eating? Even Mr. Kayankaya has to take a break sometimes—isn't that so?" She patted my shoulder.

"That's all right, Mrs. Löff. I have a lot to do today." Then, to Löff, "I need access to a couple of documents, that's all. I'm sure you can get them for me. They remember you at headquarters. What I need are the files about the two traffic accidents Vasif Ergün was in, and also, if they exist, the Narcotics Squad files on Ahmed and Vasif. It would be great if you could get me photocopies of those things. But only if you feel like doing it."

"Of course I do! At which precincts were those accidents recorded?"

"The first one happened in nineteen seventy-nine, right behind the railroad station. So it would have been that precinct."

"Right, right," he said, looking almost angry.

"The second one, the one in which Vasif was killed, took place on the twenty-fifth of April nineteen-eighty, on the road to Kronberg. I don't know exactly where, but . . ."

"I can find out. No problem."

The zeal of this grandpa of detectives was beginning to get on my nerves.

"All right. When can you have those copies for me?"

"Come back around five this afternoon."

"Will do."

Over dessert, Theobald Löff told us how, back in nineteen thirty-seven, when he was just a rookie, he had caught a Jew in the act of stealing eggs. "I was supposed to arrest him, that was my job. But you know, Mr. Kayankaya, I had heard how they were treating the Jews in those camps, so I just let him get away with it. You may say 'so what,' but do you have any idea what a risk I took? I'm sure you don't. These are different times. See, here I am, sitting at a table even with a Turk!" He laughed heartily and slapped my thigh with his shriveled old man's hand. His wife proclaimed the advantages of having one's own garden. Then I thanked them for the meal and took my leave.

Back in the Opel I had a good burp or two.

4

I parked the car in front of a games arcade and proceeded slowly down the sidewalk in the flickering heat.

A couple of my ethnic brothers stood on a corner discussing things. Otherwise it was quiet except for the noises made by pinball machines and video games. I headed toward Heini's Fried Chicken. A patrol car drove by, slowly. I pushed Heini's door open and was once again enveloped by the same weeks-old smell of grease. I sat down at a table.

It seemed my nimble friend of last night was having a day off. The waiter who now shambled in my direction looked much better suited to this stinking chicken crematorium. He had combed a few greasy strands of reddish hair across his balding pate.

"What can I get you?"

He stuck his soccer ball of a head at me as if he wanted me to pat it.

"A Scotch, a cup of coffee, and some fresh air."

"Right away."

He turned and danced off, swinging his hefty hips. He reminded me of a gay hippopotamus.

The ventilation fan started humming. I stuck a cigarette in my mouth and searched for matches. A familiar scent hit my nostrils.

"How you doing, big strong sheik?"

The young lady from Milly's Sex Bar flopped into a chair across from me. This time she was in civvies.

"Hello, darling. No purple panties today?"

She smiled. Not too much and not too little. Just right.

"I don't start work till seven. Mind if I join you? I need to eat something."

The soccer ball reappeared between us and pushed my coffee and Scotch across the table.

"What can I do for you, madam?"

"Half a chicken with fries, please."

"Half a chicken it is."

She lit a cigarette, crossed her long, tight-skirted legs, and said, "You sure made an impression in our shop. The boss and her beat-up friends spent all night trying to figure out how they could tear your head off. What happened?"

"Oh . . . I was just in a bad mood."

She flashed her white teeth at me in an ironic grin.

"Right, sure, it was all in a day's work for you, wasn't it? You just felt like wasting those two gorillas. You're a super-sheik. May I stay here, or does my mediocrity bother you?"

"Not a super-sheik, just the Fat Thing from the Kebab King."

"And that's why you beat people up?"

Her half-a-chicken fluttered onto the table and saved me from trying to think up an answer.

The french fries had a brown patina. She guided a forkful to her mouth. Before she had quite swallowed it, she asked, "Have you had any success in your search for that, that . . . what's his name again?"

"Ahmed Hamul."

"Right. How's it going with that?"

"Well, I don't have to look for him. He's dead."

"OK, I guess I meant his girlfriend, whatever . . ."

"The search goes on."

A piece of chicken trembled on the tines of her fork.

"Really feeling talkative today, aren't you?"

"Oh, dear God, there really isn't that much I can tell you. Maybe tomorrow."

"Uh-huh. And what are you doing here?" She laughed. "Are you waiting for Rudi to come off his shift?"

"Who's this Rudi? Should I know him?"

She rubbed two fries together and giggled. "That depends."

"You don't mean the waiter they forgot to give a neck?"

"He's cute, isn't he?"

"Sure. He's real sexy."

"You got a hard-on?"

"I wear leather briefs."

"Rudi insists on condoms."

"Why doesn't he take the pill?"

"He likes those ribbed ones."

"What if there's a hole in them?"

"Rudi likes taking risks."

"And see where it's got him. He looks like he'll have twins, at least."

She gnawed on a drumstick and twinkled at me. I could feel it in my toes. I lit a cigarette and blew a smoke ring that landed on her nose.

"Do you know a girl by the name of Hanna Hecht?"

"Sure."

She dropped the bone on the plate, wiped shiny puddles of brown grease off the corners of her mouth, lit a cigarette, and leaned back in her chair.

"Why do you ask?"

"Hanna Hecht was Ahmed Hamul's girlfriend. I found her last night. But that was as far as that went. Her lord and master soon made it clear to me that my presence was not appreciated."

"So? Why didn't you just beat him up?"

She grinned. A small piece of dark chicken skin stuck between two of her teeth. I told her, and she stopped grinning.

"He's tougher than all those butthead bodybuilders in your shop."

"He may well be. Is that who you're waiting for?"

"Uh-huh. Tell me, do you know how deep into the heroin business those two are?"

For a moment she stared at me with suspicion. Like a cat gazing at a visitor.

"She's a junkie, and he is small fry in that line. No big deal, as far as I know. This Turk used to hang out with her here, it probably was your Ahmed. But I don't have anything to do with any of that. You have to look for someone else."

I looked at her full, soft lips, dark eyes, almost masculine shoulders, her long, powerful legs, one of them swinging slowly back and forth, her dark purple toenails, and her narrow, slightly chapped hands—and thought—? Nothing.

A voice roared, "Check, please." Rudi swished past. The place still smelled of fried chicken. A broken muffler made the window rattle. Lightning flashed in the distance.

"But I don't want to look for anyone else. Are you here in a private capacity?"

A little later, we paid up and left.

5

A few minutes before five I departed from the quarters of Susanne Böhnisch, a.k.a. Darling, and sailed down into the street with wobbly knees and a nice warm feeling in my gut. I still wanted to speak to Hanna Hecht. Löff could wait. I went back to my car and got the Parabellum. That mustachioed fop wouldn't be able to show me the door again.

In front of Hanna Hecht's apartment door I put my ear to the keyhole. He was there, all right. I banged on the door and shouted, "Telegram!" The Parabellum felt cold in my right hand. I heard him come out of the kitchen grumbling about the doorbell. He opened the door.

At first, when he saw my shooting iron, the thin man's expression was one of surprise, then it changed into one of disgust. He did not seem to be paying any attention to the rest of me. I noticed, just in time, his hand creeping up to his armpit.

"Freeze, buster. Hands off that gun. This time it's my finger on the trigger. Turn around and put your hands behind your neck."

He made an annoyed face. As if he had spilled sour milk all over himself.

"I bet you learned that from TV, didn't you, my friend?"

That's right, I thought, but didn't admit it.

"Cut the chitchat. Turn around."

He obeyed. I pushed the black barrel of my gun into his spine, pushed him up against the wall, and retrieved his pistol from its shoulder holster. "Take it easy. Now we'll go through that door. For your sake, I hope your partner won't do anything stupid."

He growled something and walked ahead of me. As we entered the room with the horse posters, we saw Hanna Hecht standing behind the refrigerator. She was holding a small brown automatic with both hands.

"Put that down, sister, I've got a bigger one." To emphasize that fact, I waved the Parabellum in the air. That was a mistake.

Mr. Moustache shifted gears real fast and jammed his elbow into my ribs. If he had managed to get me in the solar plexus, I would have hit the linoleum like a sack of wet garbage. But he missed. I staggered back a step while he turned. Then I swung and slapped the barrel of the gun across his face. He stood there a second or two, staring past me into the void. Then his eyes went dim and he crashed to the floor, striking a shelf on the way. I turned to face Hanna Hecht. Still holding her automatic, she stared at me with wide eyes and trembling lips.

"Put that thing down, sister, or I'll blow your friend's brains out."

Slowly, as if hypnotized, she let go of the gun. It fell on the floor.

"All right. I don't enjoy acting the wild man, but there doesn't seem to be any other way to have a word with you."

I pointed at her kitchenette furniture.

"Let's sit down, and you can tell me a little about Ahmed Hamul."

She stuck her trembling hands in her jeans pockets and leaned against the window frame.

"I'd rather stand."

Her frozen face began to look stupid to me.

"As you wish."

I lit a cigarette, inhaled a little nicotine, and considered what I wanted to know.

"How long did you know Ahmed?"

She nibbled on her bloodless lower lip and didn't say anything.

"Listen, dearie, if you can't bring yourself to open your mouth, we'll just hurry on over to the nearest police precinct. Those folks are also interested in Ahmed's death. I'd rather not take you there, because I don't like them either, but if you'll just go on chewing your lips, I'll..."

"All right, all right. I'll talk to you."

She swallowed. "I knew him for about three years."

"Was he dealing when you first met him?"

"He sure was." She sounded bitter.

"You got together with him because he had the stuff?"

"That's how it started."

I pointed at half-dead Mr. Moustache.

"And what about him?"

"He worked for Ahmed, now and again."

"Quite a threesome you must have been."

"You might say that."

"Did you and Ahmed have anything going besides that business?"

"I really liked him."

"What about Mr. Moustache?"

"That's just business."

"You don't think it's possible that this guy, while he worked for Ahmed, got pissed off at him and stuck a knife in his back—do you?"

"No, that's impossible."

I believed her.

"Where did Ahmed get the stuff?"

"No idea."

"I'm asking you: where did he get the stuff?"

"And I told you. I have no idea."

"Pay attention, sister. If you don't tell me the truth, I'll take you and your buddy straight to the precinct. You hear me?"

She ran the tip of her tongue over her lips and looked at the floor. For a moment, I thought she was getting ready to act seductive. But she replied, in a bored monotone, "You ought to know, that business only works if nobody knows each other. Ahmed and I got along great—but he would never have told me who his supplier was. It would have been damn stupid of him to do that. The less you know, the less you have to tell."

Unfortunately, she was right. But I didn't believe her.

"Did you know his family?"

"He didn't talk about them very often."

"Did you know that his little sister-in-law is on the needle?"

"Yes."

"And did you know that it was he who got her on it?"

I had no idea whether that was true or not, but it was a possibility. She hesitated, then said "yes" in a quiet, choked voice. I patted myself on the back and briefly pondered the family life of the Ergüns.

"But he wanted to get her off it again. He . . ."

Her voice faded. She stared into space, lost in thought or memory. It couldn't have been easy for her, a stone addict, to talk about recovery.

"How did he intend to do that?"

"One of those sanatoriums. He had found a place for her. Something like that."

My brain came up with a brand-new thought.

"Was Ahmed planning to get out of the business?"

"Uh-huh. Yes, he was."

"What did he have in mind?"

"He wanted to take his family and move someplace else. He had a little money, and he wanted to buy a house. In another town."

"Did his family know about this plan?"

"I don't think so."

It was time for me to find out who Ahmed Hamul had been dealing with.

"The day Ahmed died—had he been here?"

"Ye-es."

She looked through the dusty window pane, down into the street. The sun was still shining out there. I looked at her bony back. Her shoulder blades stuck out from her emaciated body.

"When was he here?"

"In the afternoon."

"What time, exactly?"

She turned, and pushed her hands even deeper into her pockets, and for the first time there were some signs of lucidity in her face. She was pissed off.

"Why is that so important, you dumb sleuth?"

"It just is."

She went to the table and tore a cigarette out of a pack.

"He came here around four and left again at five thirty."

"Did he say where he was going?"

"No. He said he had to check something out."

"Some smack?"

"No, jelly babies."

"But I thought he wanted to get out of the business."

"You need some folding money to do that."

"OK. Did anyone call him here?"

"Just one of his buddies."

"His buddies?"

"All right, one of his Turks. That's what he told me, at least."

"You didn't believe him?"

"Oh, I don't know. I picked up the phone, and the guy spoke standard German. With maybe a little bit of an accent, but not much."

"Could it have been a pretend accent?"

"I have no idea."

"What was his voice like?"

"Just a voice."

"Deep? High? Nasal? Anything?"

"Listen, I only spoke to him for a second. I didn't have time to find out if he had a headache or athlete's foot."

"Ahmed spoke German with him?"

"All he said at this end was 'ja, ja'."

"When did he get the call?"

"Just before he took off."

I dug a little earwax out of my left ear, crumbled it between my fingers, waited for inspiration. Hanna Hecht nibbled her knuckles and looked at me as if I were a vacuum cleaner salesman.

There had to be some connection. Somewhere there was a person who had supplied Ahmed Hamul with heroin and who had tried to flatten me with a Fiat, or at least had pretended to do so.

And that was, in all likelihood, the same person who had killed Ahmed Hamul.

"Do you have a newspaper?"

"You plan on staying here a while?"

"I'll stay until I can't think of anything else to ask you. Come on, do you have a paper?"

"No."

I raised the Parabellum above the edge of the table.

"Let's go next door. Maybe we can find one there."

"What the hell do you want a newspaper for?"

"I want to know how my team did in the game. Let's go."

Reluctantly she walked across the kitchen and led the way through the door and across the hall into the other room. Mr. Moustache was still slumbering.

Hanna Hecht's office consisted of a bed, two metres by two metres, with a shiny sky-blue counterpane, a wardrobe, and many small chests of drawers. A stack of dog-eared porno novels lay on a white plastic table. I picked one up and looked at it.

"So the johns can use these like catalogues, like, and pick their favourite exercise?"

"The johns can go jack off too."

I put the book back on the table.

"All right, if you have any newspapers here, hand them to me."

"I don't have any"

I opened the wardrobe door and started throwing her things across the room. Hanna Hecht turned white. Her eyes gleamed. She looked like a cat, ready to pounce.

Eventually I pulled out the last stocking, and the wardrobe was empty. The floor looked like a sale table in a department store.

"Nothing there, eh?"

Hanna Hecht didn't say anything. I started shaking out the drawers of the chests. Lipsticks, hairpins, tampons, letters, sewing kits, all kinds of things spilled out of them. None of any interest to me.

Those cut-up newspapers probably weren't here. But maybe something else was. Something that would give me a clue. I did not believe that Hanna Hecht knew none of the people Ahmed Hamul dealt with, and I was hoping to find something to prove me right.

The contents of one drawer after another spread out on the claret-coloured carpet. Then I took a look at a bundle of letters, checked the postmarks. None of them were recent, and most had been mailed from Ommersbach, a small town, probably Hanna Hecht's birthplace. Relics of a time when she had still discussed skin problems with the friends of her youth.

I felt like a desecrator of graves, and put the letters aside.

"Still nothing."

She opened her mouth and said, very calmly and evenly, "If I ever get a chance to cut your dick off, I swear I'll do it." I believed her.

There was some noise in the kitchen. I took the Parabellum and Hanna Hecht and we went back to the waiter. I bonked him on the head again. We returned to the bedroom. She looked as if she didn't give a damn however many times I knocked her friend out.

I grabbed the sky-blue counterpane and added it to the stuff on the floor. She didn't crack, just stood there like a silent iron maiden. Since I couldn't tear the walls down, I proceeded to the wastebasket. Some torn paper stuck out of it. I had noticed that before.

I turned it upside down. Cigarette butts, condoms, an empty Coke can, a magazine with summer fashions, little bunches of hair, and in the middle of it all, a pile of torn newspapers. Most of them showed signs of having been attacked with scissors. I blew the ashes off them and got back to my feet.

"See here, young lady. These must have slipped your mind."

She had decided to keep her mouth shut for the rest of the day.

I spread the papers on the stripped bed and took out my notepad and a ballpoint pen. It wasn't easy, holding my shooting iron in one hand, and writing with the other. Many of the letters had been cut out carelessly, and I had to write down several possibilities. It took me almost half an hour to copy all the missing letters onto my pad. The result looked like this:

KOONERERUROTETALONANDUAILM
IMUDYHSOLIREAYOTGLLARFMFSDER

There was no way I could figure that out on the spot, but it was clear that the note addressed to me had not been composed of these particular letters. I folded the papers and stuck them in my coat pocket.

"Sister—I'm sure you do know who Ahmed's supplier was. And I think you're planning to cash in on that knowledge. A word to the wise: you might end up the way Ahmed did."

Her eyelids drooped wearily. "Shut up, you jackoff. I haven't got the faintest idea what you're talking about."

"That's all right. Do what you want. You don't have much to lose."

It was no use. I couldn't get through her defenses.

"The recipient of your glue job is bound to show up. Here, I'll leave my number. You might need some help."

I wrote my phone number on the wallpaper above her bed. That way she wouldn't immediately tear it up.

"Don't waste your time."

"Maybe it is a waste of time. Most likely I'll be wasting more time when I leave here. What I should do is stay and wait until you're ready to talk."

"Do what you want, jackoff. I don't give a shit."

"I'll find out some other way. When you're dead, at the latest. Blackmailing murderers is too big a deal for a little whore and her pimp, who isn't Arnold Schwarzenegger, exactly."

I checked my watch. A few minutes to six. Time to call Löff.

"When it begins to dawn on you that you're in it way over your head, let me know. And that's the last thing I'm telling you."

I pocketed the Parabellum and walked past her to the apartment door. I glanced into the kitchen. The waiter was still out.

"My regards to your friend, when he wakes up. See you later."

I closed the door slowly. Hanna Hecht had nothing further to say.

6

"Promptness is an indispensable prerequisite for successful work in the field of criminal investigation. I hope you don't mind my telling you that."

I felt like hanging up on him.

"Listen, Mr. Löff, I haven't been wasting my time. I'll explain later. Please tell me what you found out at headquarters. I need to know."

"I thought you were coming back here so we could go over it together."

"I can't do that now. Let's do it tomorrow."

"In this profession, it is important to familiarize oneself thoroughly with all the facts in a case. Careless haste can be damaging, and may lead to rash conclusions."

"True, true, Mr. Löff. Please, could you tell me now what it says in those files?"

He was silent for a moment. I began to worry that he might insist on my coming to his house.

"Just a minute."

He took his time. I was sure that those files lay right next to his phone. An excited guy with a small leather suitcase knocked on the door of the phone booth and waved his arm. He seemed to think that I had used up my share of time. Löff had not come back. I heaped silent maledictions on his head.

The guy pushed the door open.

"You think you own that phone?"

"Beat it."

"I beg your pardon?"

"I beg your pardon?"

Quite a chorus, Löff and this guy.

"Mr. Löff? I'm sorry, I'm having a little problem here."

I put my hand over the receiver.

"Just go find another booth! There's plenty of them."

The man slammed the door shut and shook his fist.

"You sure took your time."

"Mr. Kayankaya, I have other obligations besides doing your work for you." I didn't believe that for one minute.

"All right, then. What do the files say?"

"I could only find records of the accidents. The Narcotics Squad does not have your two candidates on its books."

"Not even their names? Who did you speak to? Was it that guy in specs with a perennial hangover?"

"It was Georg Hosch. If that's who you have in mind."

"Probably so. What does it say about the accidents?"

"The first accident occurred on the nineteenth of February, nineteen seventy-nine, at the intersection of Niddastrasse and Ludwigstrasse. The parties involved were Vasif Ergün and a certain Albert Schönbaum."

"What's his address?"

"Hold your horses! At that time Albert Schönbaum's address was Schumannstrasse twenty-three, his telephone number seventy-one fifty-eight forty. The accident re—"

"Hang on a second, I have to write that down."

I squeezed the receiver between my ear and shoulder and jotted down numbers on my pad. The receiver smelled of sweaty hands.

"All right, onward."

"The accident report is rather sketchy. It concludes that Albert Schönbaum caused the accident by driving a defective vehicle at excessive speed. The file does not go into any further detail."

"Oh, so it really says it was the other guy's fault? That's outrageous. Who reported the accident?"

Löff paused. I could hear pages being turned.

"Listen carefully. Here goes."

The old fellow seemed to be dramatizing things.

"Goes what?"

"The officers on the scene were Harry Eiler and Georg Hosch. Georg Hosch wrote the report, and Roland Futt was the officer in charge at the precinct. He signed the thing."

I squeezed the receiver against my ear.

"Oh . . . really . . ."

"Yes, siree . . . It's up to you to decide if that's just coincidence or if you want to make something of it. Personally, I don't believe that it has any bearing on the murder you're investigating. I know you don't like Futt, but you mustn't jump to rash conclusions. It might not be healthy. In the meantime, Futt has become a respected superintendent."

At the moment I had no conclusions whatsoever, rash or otherwise.

"Right . . . right. What is there on the second accident?"

"Let me warn you once more: let's have no charges of the Light Brigade here. Sometimes you get these wild coincidences."

Another pause.

"But the plot does thicken. You already know the date of the second accident. It occurred on highway B-14 between Frankfurt and Kronberg, not far from Kronberg, near kilometre marker number thirty-six. According to the report, Vasif Ergün struck a concrete pillar and rolled his car over. The car exploded and ended up in a ditch. Medical assistance arrived too late."

"You don't say. Who wrote that report?"

"At the scene were Erwin Schöller and Harry Eiler. Harry Eiler wrote the report."

"A lot of coincidences, wouldn't you say?"

"Feel free to think what you want, Mr. Kayankaya. But be careful."

"Who is Erwin Schöller?"

"I knew you'd want to know that. Until nineteen eighty-one, Erwin Schöller was a patrolman on the beat in Frankfurt. That year he asked for a transfer to Pfungstadt."

"His address?"

"Pfungstadt, Ladenstrasse three, phone ninety-five ten thirty-three."

I wrote that down. Thoughts buzzed back and forth in my brain.

Until now, I really hadn't known how to go on with the case. Now I didn't know where to begin.

"Do you know if those four—Futt, Eiler, Schöller, and Hosch—had anything to do with each other at an earlier date?"

"In nineteen seventy-five, Futt was Harry Eiler's and Georg Hosch's instructor. Futt transferred to the Narcotics Squad, and a little later he secured Hosch an appointment as his permanent assistant."

"Curiouser and curiouser. Mere coincidence, eh? Those three become inseparable. Our police force isn't *that* small—they didn't have to run into each other all the time. With due respect to the quirks of fate, Mr. Löff—"

"I know what you're trying to say, Mr. Kayankaya. But let me tell you something, as an experienced policeman: if there had been anything fishy about it, it would have come to light long ago. Not that the police force doesn't have its rotten eggs, but they don't last that long. Believe me, I know that outfit better than you do."

I scanned my notes. Futt's career had been exemplary.

"For that first accident, Futt is cited as the senior officer in charge at the precinct. But he was a member of the Narcotics Squad. What was he doing at the precinct?"

Löff seemed to be trying to find another synonym for coincidence. He couldn't come up with one.

"I have no idea. Maybe he was just visiting."

"Sure. Maybe he was taking a walk around the railroad station and wanted to use the john at the precinct. And after he had taken a leak, everybody wanted him to sign their reports. I'm sorry, Mr. Löff, but I always thought the police were sticklers for order and protocol."

"Well, by seniority Futt was entitled to sign the report."

"That's good to hear."

I realized that Löff really couldn't help me any further. I had to make some more phone calls. He made mildly offended noises and seemed reluctant to end our conversation. We made a date for the next day. That pacified him, and I hung up.

7

As I climbed the stairs to my office, I heard the phone ring. I ran the last few steps, unlocked the door in a hurry, and grabbed the phone. "Kayankaya Investigations."

He or she hung up. I listened to the crackle on the line for a moment.

It was a hot day, and the office was warm and smelly. I pulled up the blind, opened the window, and sat down at my desk with a cold bottle of beer. I took a long pull at it and thought about Susanne Bönisch, who was presently rubbing the crotches of paying gentlemen.

The bottle didn't last long, and I opened another one. I was just about to tell myself that the day had been successful enough and that I could now treat myself to an evening in front of the television set when the telephone rang again. This time the caller didn't hang up. It was Ilter Hamul.

She wanted to know if her brother was with me.

"No, he isn't here. Why do you ask?" "He came home from work at six o'clock, as usual, but as soon as he found out that you had talked with my mother this morning, he left again—without saying a word."

"Don't worry, Mrs. Hamul. Maybe he just went out for a beer. In any case, he isn't here. No reason for him to be here anyway."

I considered whether I should talk to Ilter Hamul about Ahmed's drug dealing and about her junkie sister. Could she tell me something I didn't know already? I didn't think so. I was also afraid to be the first one to tell her the bad news.

"How are things otherwise? Are you doing all right?"

"Yes, we're all right...Except that I got this bill, for Ahmed, and I don't really know what to do with it."

"What kind of a bill?"

"It's a reminder...It's about a house. But it doesn't seem right. We weren't buying a house. I can't figure it out."

"Who sent you that bill?"

"It's from Lüneburg. But it isn't really a bill, it's more like a letter. The man says he wants to remind Ahmed about the second installment on the house. I can't understand it."

"Mrs. Hamul—I'll see you tomorrow, and we can take a look at that letter together. All right? Until then, just put it away, and don't worry."

"I'll try not to."

We said goodbye. I drank and smoked, blew rings into the air, let my thoughts roam. The beer made me feel drowsy. I put my feet up on the desk and slid into a comfortable position. I soaked up the rest of the beer like a dry sponge. Then I let the bottle roll onto the floor and closed my eyes. I was half-drunk and tired. The room was pleasantly warm.

Just as darkness was slowly settling over my brain, the doorbell rang.

"Shit."

I struggled to my feet, shuffled to the door, opened it. At first I just stared at the muzzle with glazed eyes. Then I came awake, fast. In front of me stood two monsters. Both of them were wearing overalls and sturdy paratrooper boots. Their heads were covered with rubber face masks and had gas masks strapped on over those. One of them was aiming a medium sized gas cannon at my forehead, the other had his finger on the trigger of a smaller pistol. They stood there and did not say anything.

Slowly I raised my arms and took a step back into my office. Sweat burst out of my pores. My knees were knocking. I opened my mouth, but found that I was unable to make a sound.

The two just stood there, motionless.

I noticed that my muscles had begun to cramp and twitch. We stood there for about a minute. Then the one with the gas grenade launcher made a move.

He took three short steps in my direction and waved the black barrel at me, indicating that I should keep going. Cautiously, not risking a single suspicious move, I backed into the farthest corner. While he kept the barrel pointing at me, his companion closed the door and the window and pulled the blind down. Now we stood in semi-darkness.

I felt like shouting, but knew there was no one else left in the building. I considered what I might ask these two, but couldn't think of anything. They would never tell me who they were, and I'd find out soon enough what it was they wanted. I kept my mouth shut.

If the one with the cannon hadn't kept his eyes on me every second, I might have tried something foolish. After the door and window had been closed, the other one came and patted me down. I had left the Parabellum in the car. It wouldn't have been any use anyway.

"We warned you!"

Coming through the gas mask, his voice sounded metallic.

"We told you to stay out of this!"

"Who is 'we'?" I had recovered my voice.

"Why don't you think about it?"

He described a circle with the muzzle of the gun, right in front of my face. I couldn't see his face, but assumed that he was grinning. Then he pointed the barrel into the air and pulled the trigger.

There was a loud report and a shower of sparks flew across the room. The gas grenade burst and spread a dense cloud of smoke. Abrasive fumes penetrated into the farthest corners of the room. I pulled out the hem of my shirt and pressed it against my nose, closed my eyes tight, but it was no use. The concentration of tear gas was too powerful for my tiny office. Nothing short of a gas mask could have protected me.

Fluids poured out of my eyes, mouth, and nose, and that wasn't the half of it. I threw myself on the floor, beat the linoleum with my fists, tore my shirt and covered my face with it. All to no avail. I tried to get up, fell down again immediately, tried once more, and banged my elbow on the backrest of my chair. That hurt, but not a fraction as much as that damn gas was hurting my head. I banged my head against the side of the desk, but the burning fumes wouldn't go away. I screamed, roared, waved my arms. I was blinded, my eyes felt as if they had been dipped in acid.

Then they started kicking me with their paratrooper boots. They kicked me in the stomach, in the face, everywhere. I could sense their huge shadowy shapes looming above me. I had to puke.

"You leave Ahmed Hamul alone, once and for all! You understand, darkie? If you don't, we'll snuff you!"

They went on driving their boots into my body. The gas settled on my cracked skin and I tried to scrape the burning goo off with my fingernails. That didn't work. Now they were kicking me in the back, aiming for the kidneys. I was almost numb.

"If you wake up alive, you leave town. Understand?"

I forced myself to wrap my arms around my legs. I was afraid I might scratch my eyes out. At some point, they stopped. They're gone, I thought, and started crawling around the desk. I tried to get to my feet but kept sliding back down on my stomach. At last I managed to raise myself up.

They were still there. They shouted something I didn't understand. They were standing by the door, and the one with the gas gun raised it again. There was a horrendous explosion right next to me and I mustered all my remaining strength to throw myself in the direction of the door in order to avoid a direct hit. This second grenade will kill me, I thought, but at the same time I realized they had left. I fumbled around in total desperation, completely blind, until I reached the door. I threw my whole weight against the door handle. They had locked it from the outside.

I realized I was running out of air. There was no oxygen left in the room. I felt my lungs contract, reeled back the other way, to the window, and rammed my head through the glass pane. Oxygen poured in, despite the drawn blind.

After a while I was able to open my eyes. Still half-blind, I managed to find my spare key and unlock the door.

I called a doctor, gave him my office address, and passed out.

"Easy, Mr. Kayankaya, easy. You mustn't exert yourself."

I sat up carefully. I had been lying on a white cot.

"Where am I?"

"In my clinic. And you'll stay here for a while."

Two warm old eyes scrutinized me through gold-rimmed spectacles.

"I can't do that."

I heaved my legs over the edge of the bed and planted my feet on the floor.

"Well, try to get up, if you insist. You'll see what happens."

I tried, and crashed to the tiles.

"Now you want me to help you. Right?"

"No."

Slowly I dragged myself up, hanging on to the frame of the cot. I felt as if someone had extracted my spine. Nevertheless, I managed to make it to the wash basin.

"Oh my God!"

"Well, I don't know what you used to look like, but..."

What I saw in the mirror was a shapeless, pinkish-brown mess. My left incisor was broken and one of my eyes had swollen completely shut.

"You were lucky to be able to make that call. The stench was incredible. Just a couple of minutes in your office almost laid me low. But who in God's name did this to you?"

I let cold water run over my face. It felt good.

"As an emergency doctor, I see a lot of this kind of thing, but I must say they really did a job on you. Congratulations."

"Thank you."

"I see you're a private investigator. That seems to be a strenuous profession."

"Uh-huh, today was pretty strenuous."

He went to his desk and started typing something. He might as well have planted the typewriter on top of my head.

"Excuse me . . . but as long as I'm here, would you mind terribly if I asked you not to pound that machine?"

He smiled. "You see? You better admit that you're in terrible shape."

"Oh, go ahead, finish your typing."

I made my way back to the cot.

"You wouldn't happen to have a cigarette?"

"As a physician . . ."

"Do you have one or not?"

He smiled again. "Just a moment, you had some in your clothes."

He went to the corner where my pants and coat were hanging, extracted a pack, and tossed it to me.

"Thank you. A light?"

He handed me a matchbox. I lit a cigarette. For a moment I thought I'd pass out again, but then I felt better. Hungry and thirsty, in fact.

"There wouldn't be anything like a beer or a sandwich around here?"

"I'm sure we can find something. But you'll just throw up again."

"I'll risk it."

He left the room. I managed to reach my clothes and started putting them on. It wasn't easy, but not as hard as I had anticipated. The door opened and the doctor came in again. "Ham, liver sausage, cheese—whatever you fancy . . ."

He paused, looked at me.

"Now, now. How am I supposed to take this?"

"Any way you want."

"I don't care, as long as you sign a statement saying that you take full responsibility for your actions."

"I'll sign, no problem."

"If I may make a suggestion, it is this: go home and stay in bed for two or three days. That would be best."

"Will do. Starting the day after tomorrow."

I shambled over to the desk and took a small openface cheese sandwich. I bit into it, and felt just fine.

"No beer?"

"There's just one left, and that one's for me."

"All right."

I chewed my sandwich and palpated my stomach.

"No serious injuries?"

"You may have cracked a rib. If so, you'll notice. I want to see you again, in any case, within a day or two."

"Where do I sign?"

He pushed a preprinted form across the desk. I signed, and helped myself to a small ham sandwich.

"All right, then. See you later."

"You come see me the day after tomorrow."

"Will do."

"And take it easy. Another escapade like that, and you won't get off so easily."

"I'll do my best to remember that. Have a nice evening."

"You too. The bus stop's just round the corner. We are in the Westend. I don't know where you want to go."

"I do. Thank you."

8

"Schöller."

"Good evening, Mr. Schöller. My name is Kemal Kayankaya. I work for the Public Prosecutor's office. I am researching a case that you were involved in some time ago."

I had some difficulty speaking. My tongue kept hitting the broken tooth. I was holding a wet washcloth over my right eye.

"You are Erwin Schöller, correct?"

"That's me."

"Do you remember the events of the twenty-fifth of April, nineteen-eighty?"

"Not offhand, I don't. What happened then?"

"You were on patrol with a certain Harry Eiler. On that day, you reported an accident near Kronberg. Does that ring a bell?"

There was a moment's silence.

"Yes, yes it does. It does ring a bell."

"Please try to remember what happened, to the best of your ability. Tell me how you came across this accident and so on."

He cleared his throat and took his time.

"Well . . . You work for the Public Prosecutor?"

"That's right."

"Let me tell you something . . . I can't really give you any details. You see, I wasn't really there . . ."

"What exactly does that mean?"

"You see, I don't want to level any accusations, and . . ."

"It's not a question of levelling accusations."

"All right, then. This is the way it was. Back then, I had a little girlfriend in the city, you know what I mean? And Harry and I, we went on patrol together a lot of the time, and we had this agreement where he would sometimes just go on by himself while I paid my friend a visit. In return, I would type up his reports for him . . . You see, I have a wife and kids, and it wasn't easy to get away . . ."

"I understand. And on that day, you were visiting your friend?"

"Well, as a matter of fact . . . I hadn't been planning to . . . but after we got in the car, Harry asked me if I wouldn't like to take a little time off. He said he wouldn't mind, and he pointed out that I was going on vacation the following week, with the family . . . and so on. So I said, sure, why not."

"Can it cause problems if your superiors find out you do these things while you're on patrol?"

"Oh sure it can. But my girlfriend lived in the same district we covered, and whenever anything serious happened, Harry would call me, and I would just dash off . . . That was the strange thing, that day. It even struck me as strange. Harry had no business being in Kronberg, and we had to go through all kinds of contortions to keep that from getting out."

"Did Harry tell you what he was doing in Kronberg?"

"He told me it had been such a pretty day, and he had just felt like getting out into the green belt."

"Did he describe the accident to you?"

"Just that it was a bad one. Nothing else."

"Thank you for talking to me Mr. Schöller. Have a nice day."

"Is there going to be trouble because of this?"

Oh no, don't worry, Mr. Schöller. Goodbye."

I hung up quickly, before he could frame another question. I went to the sink and soaked the washcloth in fresh water. One more call, then it would be bedtime. I dialled the number I had for Albert Schönbaum. It took a while before anyone answered.

"Hello?"

"Good evening. Is this the Schönbaum residence?"

"Yes, it is. Who is this?"

"You don't know me. My name is Kayankaya. I would like to speak to Mr. Schönbaum. Are you Mr. Schönbaum?"

"No, not me. Just a minute, I'll call him to the phone."

I heard him shout "Albi". It took Albi almost five minutes to get to the phone.

"Schönbaum here."

"Good evening, Mr. Schönbaum. My name is Kemal Kayankaya. I'm a private investigator. If you don't mind, I would like to ask you a couple of questions."

"A private investigator? There's no such thing."

"Oh yes, there is. Believe me."

"All right, all right. So?"

"On the nineteenth of February, nineteen seventy-nine, you were involved in an automobile accident. Is that correct?"

"You working for an insurance company?"

"So you know the accident I mean?"

"Uh huh."

"I am not working for an insurance company, Mr. Schönbaum, so don't worry about that. All I want to know is whose fault that accident was."

"Not mine."

"But that's what it says in the police report."

"I know. That was the official story."

"What do you mean by that?"

"See, this fellow banged into my left hand door. No two ways about it. Then drove to the precinct to make the official report. But first the cops talked to the guy for a while. He was a Turk. I waited until they were done with him. Then a cop came to me and asked me if I had proper insurance, and then he wanted to know if I would agree to say that it had been my fault. At first I thought, hey, what kind of a deal is this, but then the cop explained it to me. That Turk didn't have insurance, so he would have to go to jail or would be deported, the whole sad rigmarole. And the deal was that he'd just slip me two thou, and I'd get my insurance to pay for the damages. I was pretty surprised by that offer, as you may well imagine. But who was I to complain when these cops wanted to act like human beings—for a change? End of story. The next day I went and picked up the Turk's money, and my insurance paid up. And that was it."

I too was pretty surprised.

"When you saw the Turk and he gave you the money—what did he say?"

"He was real nice to me and kept thanking me every minute. Nothing else. I had no problem understanding that. Who wants to be sent back to Anatolia?"

"Thank you, Mr. Schönbaum. Can I reach you at this number in the near future?"

"Sure. Why do you ask?"

"I may call you again. Until then, take care."

"Yeah, likewise."

I turned the radio down low, on the classical station, switched off the light, and went to bed.

DAY THREE

I

Four grey concrete pillars rose up against the sky. They didn't make any sense. A couple of birds seemed to be using them as a rest stop, but that was all. At some time they must have been intended as supports for a bridge. The bridge had never been built.

I dragged myself out of the Opel and walked over to the pillar on the far right. Traces of the paint job of Vasif Ergün's red car were still visible on it. The ditch lay two metres to the side, and immediately behind the pillars stood the first houses of Kronberg, facing vast potato fields. I walked a hundred metres to the first bungalow and pressed the bell button next to the garden gate. A curtain moved, and the front door opened a moment later.

"What do you want?"

"My name is Kemal Kayankaya. I am a private investigator. I would like to ask you a question. Just one."

She stood there, undecided. I did not look all that inviting. My face was still quite swollen, and half of it was covered with a dark crust. My chest also hurt like hell, but she couldn't see that.

"A private investigator?"

She was wearing a dark blue jogging suit and looked to be around forty.

"It's an odd profession, I know."

She came to the gate, slowly, her clogs clattering against the flagstones.

I smiled. I'm sure I looked horrible. She leaned against the gate.

"And it is?"

"What?"

"Your question?"

She was quite heavily made up. She looked at me with suspicion.

"Four years ago an accident happened here, or about a hundred metres from here, over there by those concrete pillars. Do you remember?"

"When that Turk ran into one?"

"That's right. Did you happen to be at home that day?"

"Yes, I was. But I didn't see anything. I was in the backyard gardening."

"Do you know anybody who lives here or used to live here who saw exactly what happened?"

"No . . . those things happen so fast. We heard the explosion, all of us . . . but as for the rest—wait a minute."

She raised her index finger to her lips and thought for a moment.

"There was somebody who saw it. The eldest daughter of Hornen the farmer over there."

She pointed at a farmhouse across the way.

"But she died."

"She died?"

"Yes, yes, I remember now. Very soon after the accident, a roof tile fell on her head and killed her. She was accident-prone, she was."

"But she had seen the crash?"

"Yes, she saw it. And she got a lot of mileage out of it too."

"How do you mean?"

"Well, she just started acting important, the way farm-girls like to do. In places where nothing ever happens, whenever something does, like that accident, right in front of your doorstep, people tend to make a big deal of it."

"What did she say about it?"

"Oh, it was just crazy talk. She claimed it hadn't been an accident. She said there had been another car that ran the Turk off the road. Something like that. It sounded like complete nonsense. The police got to the scene very soon after, and they checked it all out. They would have noticed if there had been any signs of foul play."

"And the girl was killed very soon after that?"

"The next day, in the evening. It was tragic, all right."

I looked over to the farmhouse. "Do you think Mr. Hornen is in?"

"Oh, I'm sure he is."

"I think I'll have a word with him. Many thanks for your help. Have a good day."

"'Bye."

She clip-clopped back to her bungalow.

Hornen ran a clean farm.

There wasn't a single piece of kindling, no pile of straw, not even any dog shit on the swept flag stones of the yard. The stable sported a new door, and the shutters were freshly painted. Some kind of wrought iron emblem hung above the front door. Blooming flowerboxes adorned the windowsills.

I knocked on the door. A dog started barking.

"Who's there?"

I repeated my little spiel, and soon the farmer stood before me.

"Mr. Hornen?"

"The same."

"I would like to ask you a question about your daughter. The one who passed away four years ago."

"Go ahead."

"How exactly did she die?"

"Roof tile fell on her head."

"Where?"

"Two houses down, to your left."

"When exactly did it happen?"

"February twentieth, nineteen hundred seventy-nine, seven o'clock at night."

"Did she die immediately?"

"Yes, she did."

"What did the doctor say?

"Roof tile killed her."

"Could you tell me the name of the doctor?"

"Langner. To your left, third street on the right, second house on the left."

"Thank you."

"You're welcome."

He closed the door.

I walked back to the pillars, got into my Opel, and drove over to Dr. Langner.

"Private investigator?"

I pocketed my license again.

"That's right."

"Please come in."

He led the way across his waiting room to the office. After I had given my card to the nurse who opened the door and she had taken it to Dr. Langner, he had come to the door himself. While we passed through the waiting room his patients gave me sympathetic looks. My face indicated that I was an urgent case.

"What can I do for you?"

"Four years ago, you issued a death certificate for Farmer Hornen's daughter. Am I right about that?"

"Yes, you are. Why do you ask?"

"I would like to know if it was roof tile or a brick that killed the girl. Or if there was any doubt about that."

He shifted his weight in his chair.

"I have no idea why you want to ask me that. But you must have your reasons." A pause. "There were doubts—but they were all mine. Everybody in the family and the community was sure it had been a roof tile, so that's what I wrote on the death certificate. You may criticize me for that, if you wish. But even if I had voiced my doubts, it wouldn't have led to anything."

He seemed touchy about his professional integrity. But he also seemed honest.

"What do you think the more likely cause of death was?"

"To judge from the skull fracture, it had to have been a heavy bar or log. Not just a single roof tile. The fracture ran straight across the bone; it was too long to have been caused by a tile."

"Was the tile ever found?"

"It lay right next to her, among many others. They were putting new tiles on that roof."

"Would you be willing to admit to the error in court, and testify under oath to the cause of death you find appropriate?"

He stared at his hands for a long while. Then he looked up again.

"Yes, I would be willing to do that."

2

"OK, then. I'll meet you at headquarters in twenty minutes. Can you get hold of a cassette recorder by then?"

"What do you need a cassette recorder for?"

"Rare birdsongs. But it has to be one that runs on batteries."

"I'll try, I think we have one of those somewhere. I'll check with my wife."

"And hurry up."

"All right, all right."

Half an hour later Löff's blue Mercedes turned into the parking lot at police headquarters. I walked across the gravel to greet him as he emerged from the car carrying a shiny black briefcase. He was wearing a suit and tie.

"Good morning, Mr. Löff. Did you find a recorder?"

He pulled an ancient little thing out of his briefcase. I took it and tested it. The recording quality was far from impressive, but it would do for my purposes. I handed it back to Löff.

"You hang on to it for now. We won't need it quite yet."

"Mr. Kayankaya, how about if you'd be so kind as to explain, at long last . . ."

"No way. I can't explain anything to you yet. Either you help me without asking a lot of questions—or forget the whole thing."

"How can we work together if you don't tell me anything?"

"I think we can work together just fine."

"How so?"

"Listen, Mr. Löff, at this point all I need is your name. It has a lot more prestige in official circles than mine does. This will become evident right here at headquarters. If you go in there with me, they won't kick me out again, and they might even answer my questions. If I start explaining to you what it is I need to know and why, we'll be standing here for hours, and we don't have that much time anymore. I'm sorry, but that's the way it is."

"Mr. Kayankaya, if I may give you some advice, based on my experience . . ."

"Are you ready to help me or not?"

He glared furiously at me for a second. Then he snapped the briefcase shut with a defiant expression.

"All right. Where do we start?"

"We'll pay another visit to the Narcotics Squad, and one to the armory."

"Let's go."

We crossed the parking lot, walked up the stairs to the main entrance and hall, and took the elevator to the fourth floor.

In front of Georg Hosch's office I grabbed Löff's arm.

"Not Hosch. We have to find someone else."

"Why?"

"Because!"

Löff took a deep breath, then pointed to the door facing Hosch's office.

"You go in and perform the customary salutations. I ask the questions."

Löff knocked energetically.

"Step right into the parlour."

The friendly voice belonged to a young lady in a miniskirt who was spooning coffee into a filter. Löff entered the room with the relaxed dignity of a superior officer. He did it well. Unfortunately, the miniskirt did not seem impressed by dignified superiors.

"Whoever it is you want to talk to—they're all gone."

She switched on the coffeemaker and turned to look at us. Löff crossed his arms over his chest.

"I am Theobald Löff, detective superintendent, retired."

"Yes, and?"

"I wish to speak to the man in charge of the department."

"Mr. Rolland is out on official business."

"When do you expect him back?"

"God alone knows."

Löff had finished his performance. He turned to me questioningly.

"My name is Kayankaya. Do you know the workings of this squad except for where they keep the coffee?"

"I should think so. I've been here for two years."

"There is a depository where all the confiscated dope is kept before they burn it at some later date. Where is that?"

"There's one out by the airport, a kind of halfway house, and the main depository is here at headquarters. They burn it in a special furnace in the back courtyard."

"Who has access to that depository here at headquarters?"

"Hey, you're not planning to rob the place, are you?"

"Sure. I just walk into the first cop shop in town and ask where and how I . . ."

"Enough, enough. The only person who has access is a trustee who unlocks the place when they bring in some new stuff and keeps tabs on what's in there."

"What's his name?"

"At the moment, it is Mr. Sörbier. But it rotates, every month."

"Is he also in charge of the cremations?"

"No, those are always done by Mr. Hosch."

"Georg Hosch?"

"That's right."

"Mr. Kayankaya, please, what's the deal here? You can't go on leaving me completely in the dark."

We stood in the elevator on our way down to the basement. I fingered my broken rib. The next day I would start taking care of it. Or so I hoped.

"There's no other way, Mr. Löff. Tonight you'll know everything. Please be patient until then. You did really well back there. Excellent job."

"All right, I'll go along. But could you do me a favour?"

"What is it?"

"Try to acquire a few manners, my dear man. There are ways of talking to people without instantly offending them. Next time, say 'thank you' and 'goodbye' when you have received the desired information. After all, your behaviour reflects on me."

The elevator doors opened and saved me from having to reply to that. We walked across a hall that was lit by fluorescent fixtures and up to what looked like a kiosk. Behind it, instead of cases of beer and candy, was a huge room filled with metal shelves.

These in turn were filled with olive-green articles of clothing, Plexiglas shields, helmets, traffic control signs, shoes, all kinds of firearms, walkie-talkies, even bundles of whistles, all of it in relatively good order, all of it clean and new.

I pushed a silver-plated bell. In the back of the room a voice growled "just a moment". Löff gave me a critical look. He seemed to be still waiting for some response to his request.

"I'll try my best not to drool or burp without being asked."

"What's up?"

A small, wrinkled man came limping toward us, peering at us through thick lenses. Löff cleared his throat and put his hands on the counter.

"Oh, it's you, Superintendent. What brings you here?"

"Well, once a bear gets hooked on garbage there's no cure."

"Oh, so you're back in harness?"

"Not really. I'm just helping out with a case. To pass on what I learned in my long years on the job to my juniors. Like an ambulatory advice machine, you might say."

The little guy laughed heartily.

"That was well put, Superintendent."

Löff stepped to one side and introduced me.

"Here is one of the up-and coming, if I may say so. Mr. Kayankaya is helping us with a case."

The myopic eyes scanned me incredulously. He was probably thinking that the police force must have fallen on hard times if its up-and-coming members consisted of Turks covered in dried blood. Löff's story struck me as both unimaginative and lacking in credibility.

"I see. Well, then. What can I do for you?"

To keep Löff from spouting any more nonsense, I elbowed him aside and stepped up to the counter.

"Do you keep records of the equipment people check out here?"

"Of course I do. This is all highly regulated."

"Can an officer obtain replacements for missing items of his equipment—if, say, he has lost something, or something got damaged while he was on duty?"

"Of course, as long as he has the authorization of a superior officer. Why do you think I'm here, otherwise?"

He smiled a little at the silliness of these young whip-persnappers.

"So for instance, if I were to ask you if, during the week immediately following the twentieth of February, nineteen seventy-nine, one or several colleagues obtained a new nightstick from your supplies, you could verify that for me?"

I glanced quickly at Löff. He looked nonplussed, just as I had expected.

"No problem, except you may have to wait a moment while I find the records."

"We'll be glad to wait."

The little man limped away. Löff tapped me on the shoulder.

"Otherwise you're all right, Mr. Kayankaya?"

"Just wait and see."

We stood there in silence until the gnome returned with a light brown wooden box under his arm.

"This is the one for nineteen seventy nine. Let's see now."

He started going through the cards.

"Nightsticks, you said?"

"Right."

After a while he pulled out two cards.

"Here we are. February twenty first and February twenty-ninth. In both cases, nightstick lost while on duty, application for replacement. Authorizations from superior officers in both cases."

He looked up.

"Will that do?"

"I would like to know the names of the applicants."

"No problem."

He raised the cards up to the thick lenses.

"On the twenty-ninth, the applicant was Michael Kuch of mobile task unit D dash A seventeen twenty-one. On the twenty-first, it was Harry Eiler, patrolman, number zero zero eight dash seven three. The superior officers were, in the first case, Chief Superintendent Norbert Rutel, in the second, Detective Superintendent Futt."

I looked at Löff and said, "Many thanks. You have been a great help. 'Bye now."

We left the building and walked out onto the parking lot. Löff was still sulking and didn't say a word.

"Mr. Löff, please get your car. I'll be up there by the phone booth. I have to check an address."

I turned the thin, torn pages of the phone book. Löff had already pulled up in his Mercedes when I found what I had been looking for. Futt, Grosse-Nelken-Strasse thirty-seven. That was in Hausen, a suburb of Frankfurt. I got in next to Löff and we drove off. The large automobile rolled smoothly down the street.

"To Hausen. Grosse-Nelken-Strasse thirty-seven."

"What will we be doing there?"

"Is Futt married?"

Löff slowed down a little.

"Don't tell me you—"

"Yes. Is he married or not?"

"He is."

"So we won't have to break in."

"We won't have to *what*?"

We came to a squealing halt by the curb. Löff turned off the engine.

"Once more, and slowly. We won't do what?"

"Take it easy. We're going to Futt's apartment to have a few words with his wife. That's it. Nothing to it. You stay in the car."

"I must not have heard you right."

We got going again. I rolled down the window and held my hand out into the rushing air.

"Do you know the lucky lady?"

"No, I don't."

"Ever hear anything about her?"

"Yes."

"What did you hear?"

"Rumours."

"What kind?"

"When Futt was the head of the Narcotics Squad, there were rumours that his wife was an alcoholic. Silly gossip."

"How so?"

"Just because talk like that is always silly gossip."

"I see."

Not much later we pulled up in front of number thirty-seven.

"Why don't you find another place to park, a little farther away? But you have to be able to keep an eye on that front door. I'll be back in half an hour, if not before. Should a familiar face appear before then, hit the horn twice. That's all for now. See you soon."

I slammed the car door shut. Futt lived in a green stucco apartment building dating from the Fifties. I rang the bell. The door buzzed, and I walked up to the second floor. A brass plate bore the engraved name Paul Futt. The apartment door was ajar.

"I'm in here, Horstilein!"

I went in. The entrance hall was full of old and expensive furniture that didn't match. A sunset with a sailboat hung on the wall. The floor was covered with three or four layers of Persian carpets.

"In here, in the bedroom. Tee hee!"

I proceeded through the entrance hall to the bedroom. For a moment, we stared at each other in utter confusion. She was blown away because I was not her Horstilein but a Turk with a battered face. I was blown away because what I saw in front of me was a fat, garishly made-up woman who lay on the bed spreading her legs wide, naked except for a golden silk scarf.

"Kayankaya's the name. How do you do, madam."

Slowly, staring at me all the while, she covered up her white body with a bed sheet. On a night table stood the silly old rumour: a half-empty bottle of Johnny Walker.

"I need to talk to you. I'll step outside while you put on some clothes."

I grabbed the bottle, went out into the hall, and sat down on a sofa upholstered in silk. Late eighteenth century was my guess. I treated myself to a drink at Futt's expense. His wife was getting dressed in the bedroom. Five minutes later she stood in the doorway. Her obese body shook and her eyes were glazed. She looked more than a little smashed.

"Who are you? What do you think you're doing here?"

I set the bottle down on the floor and got up.

"As I said before, Kayankaya's the name. I've come to ask you a couple of questions."

She had put on a white kimono embroidered with dragons. Her right breast hung out of it.

"Who gives you the right to bust into my apartment?"

"I rang the bell and you buzzed me in."

She waved her hands in the air.

"So what? I was expecting a friend. How was I to know some stranger would just walk in here? You can't do that! I'm expecting a dear friend, and you just walk in, just like that. You can't do that!"

The alcohol made her rather repetitious.

"You're Paul Futt's wife, correct?"

"What do you mean by that? Did that asshole send you here? He knows all about it. He doesn't give a shit. I'm a woman, right? That impotent bag of lard is no use to me anymore. I have a right, don't I? I have a right to a little fun. How could I know he was such a washout? No one told me that in church. How could I know. I have a right..."

She covered her face with her hands and burst into sobs.

"Mrs. Futt, I don't care a damn if you have a lover or not. That's not what I'm here for."

"Fucking! Why don't you just say it, you asshole? That's what's on your mind!"

"Mrs. Futt, I don't care *who* you fuck!"

She laughed hysterically. I took her arm and sat her down on the sofa.

"Pull yourself together. Now, tell me which is your husband's room."

She stopped laughing and gave me a conspiratorial look.

"Are you from the police? Are you for him—or against him?"

"How am I supposed to understand that?"

She pulled back quickly.

"Nothing to understand. I don't know anything. I don't know anything at all!"

"I'm against him, if you wish."

"No, no, never mind. I don't know anything. He'd kill me. He told me so."

"Your husband?"

No, Santa Claus. Tee-hee!"

"Why would he kill you?"

Her lacquered nails curled around my arm. Then she pushed her ass against me and rested her boozy head on my shoulder. She smelled of an unsuccessful blend of Scotch and eau de cologne.

"You ask a lot of questions, don't you?"

Her hand slid across my navel and down. I let it slide, tongued her ear, and whispered, "That asshole's making a lot of money selling dope, isn't he?"

She giggled. "You really are something... tee-hee..."

I did my best to play up to her.

"But if they ever found out about it, you would have to tell them what you know."

"He'll kill me." She giggled.

"He can't kill you when he's behind bars."

"Swine like him never end up behind bars... Never mind him now, he's not important."

She was having trouble with the buttons.

"All right. Just tell me where he keeps his stash."

"I saw some once, in his wardrobe. That's all."

I tore myself from her embrace and got up. She looked at me, dumbfounded. I slapped her face.

"Where's the wardrobe?"

"Oh, you bastard—"

I slapped her again.

"Time to sober up. Where's the wardrobe?"

She held her cheek with one hand, and pointed at a door across the hall with the other. The wardrobe stood in the other bedroom. I cleared out coats and suits until I saw a backpack in the far left-hand corner. I pulled it out and undid the buckles. The top layer consisted of all sorts of camping paraphernalia. I turned it upside down, and among the enamel pots, gas containers, tent hooks, and nylon ropes, a number of small plastic-wrapped packages tumbled on the floor. I picked one up, tore off a corner, licked the plastic. Sure enough. After I had stuffed it all back in, I saw the folded note: MURDERER FUTT, GET A MILLION AND A KILO READY; YOU'LL HEAR FROM US SOON! I pocketed the note and stepped back into the hall. Futt's wife was huddled on the sofa, weeping.

"...nothing, disgusting, I'm disgusting."

"Where's the phone?"

She looked up at me. Her black mascara was smeared all over her face.

"...in the kitchen..."

I consulted the phone book, found the number, dialled. Hanna Hecht's number was busy. I had no time to lose.

"You stay right here until I get back, all right? A colleague of mine will be here in a minute, and he'll stay with you. It's for your own protection. Wipe that dirt off your face and make him a cup of coffee. And don't try any hanky-panky with him. See you later."

I ran downstairs and across the street. Löff was sitting in his car, listening to the radio. "Mr. Löff, things are heating up."

"Oh yeah?"

"Mrs. Futt is up there, not feeling all that good. Go to her and stay with her until I get back. Watch her closely, she might do something crazy. If Futt happens to come by, hold him there. I don't care how you do it." I handed him my Parabellum. "Here, just in case. Don't look at me like that. You may not believe it, but I have my reasons. Take a look at Futt's wardrobe."

"Is that all?"

"Yes, that's all for now. All I need is an hour. If it takes longer, I'll call. I need your car."

He handed me the keys, stuck the Parabellum in his pocket, and walked over to number thirty-seven.

I started the Mercedes and drove off. I was doing sixty through the first red light.

3

To keep my hands free, I set the cassette recorder on the floor to the left of Hanna Hecht's apartment door. I bent down to the keyhole and heard murmuring voices. I rang the bell. The murmuring stopped. I rang again. Silence. After the third ring, someone came to the other side of the door.

"Who is it?"

I recognized the voice.

"Main Gas Company. Meter reading."

"Just a moment."

A few brief whispers. Then he came back. I flattened myself against the wall to the right of the door. A key was inserted into the lock and turned, slowly. Then the door opened and he stuck his head out.

I struck him just below the belt with the edge of my right hand. That winded him for a moment, and I jumped him. Since I hadn't hit him all that hard, he put up some resistance. My first impression had been correct: he was a hair-puller. When he tried to bite my belly I decided I was fed up and punched him in the chin. He went limp and fell back on the fluffy rug. I glanced at the door to the kitchen. Hanna Hecht was staring at me with wide eyes. Her face was bruised and swollen, and her nose was bleeding. Her blouse was smeared with blood and torn open to the waist. I unwound the length of wire that had been used to tie her hands. It left bloody tracks on her arms. Then I used the same wire to tie him up. I wound it tight, and the pain revived him.

"Take it easy. It's all over now."

I turned him on to his back and stared at his face. Defenseless now, he looked like a dachshund. I noticed, too late, that Hanna Hecht had gotten down on her knees next to me. She raked her fingernails across his face. I pushed her away, a little pointlessly, since five deep scratches had now laid the raw dermis of his cheeks open. He screamed and squirmed with pain. Hanna Hecht smiled. Only now I noticed that he had smashed all of her upper incisors.

"Where is your friend from Heini's Fried Chicken?"

She pointed at the kitchen.

"Still alive?"

"More or less."

"Can you get me a drink? We could all use one now." She nodded and went to the kitchen. I took hold of his shoulders and raised him to a sitting position against the wall.

"So, Mr. Eiler, we meet again."

I got the cassette recorder from the landing and wound the tape back.

"I am going to ask you a couple of questions. You may answer; you may also refuse to answer. In the latter case, I'll hand you over to Miss Hecht to deal with you as she pleases . . . all right?"

"No! I'll talk."

"In a way, I'm sorry to hear that."

I pushed the recording button.

"How did you manage to persuade Vasif Ergün, after his automobile accident, to deal heroin that you provided him with?"

He gave me a frightened look. "But . . ."

"Let's hear it. The tape's running."

He hemmed and hawed a while before he came clean.

"Oh, what the hell, it's all over, isn't it . . . It was Futt's idea. I didn't have anything to do with that . . . I'm telling you the truth . . ."

"I don't care whose idea it was. I want you to tell me what happened."

"Well . . . We told him this had been a pretty bad accident, and he would have to go back to Turkey, or spend a long time in jail . . . something like that . . . and then we offered him a deal. We would make sure that nothing bad happened to him, we'd even give him the money to pay for the damage."

"Two thousand marks?"

"Yeah, that's how much it was . . . So we did that for him. In return, he would deal drugs for us. We offered him thirty percent of the profits, and he agreed."

"And after he'd been dealing for a while, you asked him if he knew somebody else who might be interested in dealing."

"Right."

"And that was Ahmed Hamul?"

"Yes."

"Why did you kill Vasif Ergün?"

"But—no—that was an accident . . . Surely you don't believe . . ." His voice almost cracked.

"Stop playacting. Futt has confessed, and I have a witness for the accident. It'll be to your advantage to tell the truth."

He gave a visible start at the mention of Futt's confession.

"That—that stupid swine . . . It was him, he said we had to do that, he said our cover would be blown if we didn't . . . That swine . . . I'm not a murderer, goddamn it—believe me."

He screamed and sobbed and beat his tied hands against his mutilated face; a steady tremor shook his slight body.

"Pull yourself together. You've killed three people, and you have subjected three other people to bestial torture, myself included. You weren't weeping then. You probably even enjoyed it. I'd like to tear you limb from limb, believe you me. Now you'll answer my questions—or else!"

"...he wanted to get out, he wanted to get into business on his own..."

"And that was when you ran him off the road, into that concrete pillar?"

"Yes."

"How did you know that the farmer's daughter saw what happened?"

"I made the accident report. The people came out from the village...to see what had happened...And she came too, and she started running off at the mouth about it...but no one believed her..."

"And you went back the next day and cracked her skull with your nightstick. Where is that nightstick now?"

"...I tossed it..."

"Where?"

"...can't remember..."

I backhanded him on his torn cheek. He screamed.

"...somewhere in the woods...in back of the village..."

"The drugs were provided by Georg Hosch, after the monthly burnings?"

"Yeah..."

"And last night it was you and he who came to my office and tear-gassed me?"

"Yeah..."

"The drugs were kept at Futt's house?"

"Yeah, right. It was his idea, all of it. He blackmailed us, practically, he—"

"I don't care. Why did you have to kill Ahmed Hamul?"

"I had nothing to do with that! I don't know anything about it...You can't pin everything on me ... I didn't do it...none of us did that... I would know. You can't pin that on us!"

I kept slapping his face, but he kept denying that they had had anything to do with Ahmed's murder.

"Well, we can find out what you were doing that night. Where is Hosch now?"

"On duty."

I switched off the tape and went to the kitchen. Hanna Hecht was leaning back in a chair; having just shot up, she looked relatively content. The waiter lay under the sink, groaning. He had been through a lot the last couple of days. I grabbed his shoulders to help him up, but he screamed like a stuck pig. Harry Eiler must have broken both his arms. I let him lie there, realizing that anything else might kill him outright. The kitchen looked like a battlefield. Broken furniture and dishes were spattered with blood, the garbage can had been emptied out on the floor, and all the posters had been torn off the wall and shredded. I got the vodka bottle out of the refrigerator and took a long pull. The waiter groaned out loud.

"You want a hit?"

With difficulty, he moved his eyelids up and down. I gave him a couple of spoonfuls. Most of it dribbled down his chin. Then I went back to Harry Eiler and the telephone.

I dialled Medical Emergency and called for an ambulance. Then I turned to the heap of misery that was Eiler.

"Now you will call Hosch and make a date with him. You tell him to come to Futt's apartment in half an hour."

He shook his head. I slapped him. He nodded.

"The number?"

He gave it to me. I dialled and held the receiver for him. "Yes, George . . . ? This is Harry . . . Yes, listen, we have to meet at Paul's place in half an hour . . . Yes, it is important What? . . . I can't explain on the phone, but it really is urgent . . . All right? See you then."

I hung up. Harry Eiler stared at his fettered hands with a pained expression.

"And now the same thing with Futt."

"No! . . . All right, all right!"

"You can't back out now. He has to come there. Tell him something went wrong here. I don't care."

"Paul? . . . Yes, it's Harry . . . This is really urgent . . . things didn't work out here . . . I have to see you, as soon as possible, at your place . . . yes . . . believe me, it's important . . ."

He gave me an imploring look. I shook my head.

"Paul, please, it won't take long . . . No, I'm not trying to mess with your head . . . it won't take long . . . You'll be there in half an hour? All right? OK, see you there."

I took the phone and dialled Futt's home number.

"Katrin Futt speaking."

"Hello, Mrs. Futt. Let me have a word with your guard there."

Löff came to the phone.

"This is me, Kayankaya . . . no, I'll be there very shortly . . . it's all working out. But listen, I need someone from the

Public Prosecutor's office . . . right! Can you get him there in a hurry?"

Harry Eiler started howling. I took the phone into the bedroom.

"Who is that? You won't believe this, but it's Harry Eiler . . . I'll explain. Can you do that, get a prosecuting attorney? I'm sure you have a good buddy in that line . . . I'm dead serious. I'll make him a present of three heroin dealers, and one of them is a multiple murderer. How's that for an offer?... Yes, I've got evidence. Your cassette machine was a great help . . . Fine, Mr. Löff, you may never speak to me again if this doesn't pan out . . . I need that prosecutor! Right now! For one thing, I didn't feel like telling the same story twice . . . All right, I'll be there in ten minutes."

4

Just as I was leaving the building with Harry Eiler, the emergency ambulance arrived, and two paramedics rushed out of it. One of them grabbed my arm.

"First floor on the right. The girl is full of heroin, the guy is full of vodka."

He looked at me thunderstruck. Then he nodded and charged inside.

I stuffed Harry Eiler into the passenger seat, got behind the wheel, and drove off.

Ten minutes later, there were five us sitting in Futt's living room: Katrin Futt, Theobald Löff, Harry Eiler, myself, and one Horst a.k.a. "Horstilein" Schramm. I told Katrin Futt's back-door man to take a powder. "No, I'm staying. I can't leave Katrin in the lurch like this."

"Mr. Schramm. Very shortly, things will be going on here that are none of your damn business."

"But I can't leave Katrin alone! Who are you, anyway? You haven't told me anything."

"I don't have time to argue with you. Either you leave under your own steam, or I'll kick you out! Just ask my buddy here, I'm not the squeamish type. So stop playing the gallant knight and hit the tiles!"

He looked at Harry Eiler's visage in disgust.

"Yes, it certainly looks like you're a real brute, doesn't it? I don't see how you can subject a lady to this sort of thing!"

"And you think you're helping her by sitting on your ass and complaining!"

"She needs me!"

Katrin Futt had managed to sober up a few degrees:

"Horst—I think it'll be better if you leave now. I'll see you tonight."

"But Katrin! You can't do this to me!"

I grabbed hold of his shoulder.

"Sure she can. I'll count to three. One ..."

He shook my hand off, cast a grim look around the room, and left the apartment.

"When did you say the prosecutor will get here?"

"As soon as he's able."

We sat there in a silence only sporadically interrupted by Harry Eiler's whimpering. He was disfigured for life, and why hadn't I saved him from that witch . . . For about ten minutes, no one else said a word. Löff looked as if he were sure he'd regret having called the prosecutor. Katrin Futt had closed her eyes and was sleeping off the drink. After a while, Harry Eiler decided to restrict himself to staring at his wired wrists and suffering in silence. I occupied my mind with trying to piece together a certain Louis Armstrong tune. Then the doorbell rang.

Everybody gave a start, as if they hadn't expected anything to happen ever again. I slipped the safety off the Parabellum, told the others to stay put, and went to the door.

After the second ring I threw the door open. Before Georg Hosch was able to get the picture, I stuck the black barrel of my gun in his chest, grabbed his lapels, and pulled him inside.

"I told you we'd meet again."

"What do you think you're doing?"

"Wait and see. Where's your gas mask today? You looked good in it."

He pursed his lips contemptuously. "This will have serious consequences."

"You bet it will."

I pushed him into the living room.

"Soon we'll have a quorum."

Georg Hosch remained calm. Only his forehead turned pink.

"Have a seat. We'll have to wait a few more moments until Superintendent Futt and the prosecutor get here."

"The prosecutor . . ."

"Things have a way of happening sooner than we expect, Mr. Hosch."

His only response was a disdainful stare.

A little later the doorbell rang again. I went through the same routine, throwing the door open and pushing my cannon into a chest.

This time it was the prosecutor. He looked just as flabbergasted as Hosch. I lowered the gun and apologized.

"That's all right. At least I seem to be in the right place. This is Mr. Futt's apartment, isn't it?"

"So it is."

"And where is he?"

"He hasn't arrived yet. Why do you ask?"

"Because I consider it an impertinence, to make me rush here in this heat and at this time of day! What's wrong with bringing the criminals he's apprehended to my office? Since when don't the police have the means and the time to bring their prisoners to court? I'm making this exception only because I know Mr. Löff and hold him in great esteem . . ."

"Mr. Futt will be here any minute."

"And who are you?"

"Kemal Kayankaya, private investigator. I have made you rush through town at this hour, because I am not a policeman and don't have the means to transport my prisoners to court. Mr. Futt will not appear here in his capacity as detective superintendent, but in his role as a heroin dealer. As soon as he gets here, I'll lay it all out for you. And if you find my story convincing, as I am sure you will, you can then issue the arrest warrants."

"You've said a mouthful, young man."

"I'm afraid you won't feel too good about it. All three persons concerned are members of our police force."

He ran his fingers through his short grey hair.

"I see. Well. It won't make things easier."

He scrutinized me closely.

"So when do we start?"

"We're waiting for Mr. Futt."

"The others are present?"

"Come and see."

The prosecutor's arrival had upped the tension level in the room. George Hosch was beginning to lose his cool, looking daggers at Harry Eiler, who was awash in whimpering self-pity. Katrin Futt had slowly become conscious of the situation and fidgeted in her chair.

Löff and the prosecutor exchanged greetings like people who are members of the same bowling club. Then they sat down quietly next to each other, crossed their arms over their chests, and cast the occasional impatient glance in my direction.

"Mrs. Futt, may I offer the gentlemen something to drink?"

"Yes, of course, the cabinet's in the kitchen. And the glasses are there too."

"Mr. Hosch, would you like to assist me?"

As soon as both of us were in the kitchen, I closed the door quietly and smiled at Hosch's cold eyes. His expression seemed to indicate that he thought I was an idiot.

"Listen, Hosch—let's make a deal."

"What kind of deals can you offer me?"

"For one thing, I could leave you out of my description of the tear gas attack. That would save you the charge of grievous bodily harm."

"I'm sorry, but I don't quite get your drift."

"I could arrange things so you wouldn't figure in the murder plots. Wouldn't it suit you just fine to claim that you didn't know anything about them? Poor Georg Hosch, unwittingly involved in the criminal machinations of a superior who either pressured or conned him into stealing confiscated drugs. No charges for conspiracy to commit three murders. Merely a question of a basically honest man whose simple-mindedness was exploited by others for their criminal activities. I know you won't particularly like that role, but it could save you a few years behind bars."

"Do I have to listen to any more of this nonsense?"

"It isn't nonsense, and you know it. Here's my offer: I'll begin my story with Vasif Ergün's first accident. You'll play dumb and pretend this is the first you've heard of it. I'm sure you can think of something—maybe you thought you were working for the secret service, something like that? I'll run the whole movie.

"You'll get more and more excited, act positively horrified, present a state of confusion and despair. You may even start raging at Futt, if you like. You keep that up until I get to Ahmed Hamul. At that point, you'll see the light. This is what I want from you: during the description of the third murder, you arrive at the realization that it's all true, that those two really have been deceiving you for three long years. And that's where you'll lose it completely. Because until then you have still suspected that my narrative is just some private dick's fantasy—but when I get to Ahmed Hamul's death, you realize that I am telling the truth. Get the picture?"

Hosch shook his head, but without conviction.

"Think it over. A bit of theatre, that's all. Conspiracy to commit murder and grievous bodily harm are unpleasant charges. And we needn't have any scruples about Eiler. In court, it won't matter whether he committed his atrocities alone or whether he had some help on occasion. One way or the other, he'll take the heaviest rap."

A brief grin flashed across his face. It seemed to amuse him that I thought he might have scruples about Harry Eiler.

"Better make up your mind, and soon. Now we'll serve the folks some drinkies."

I got the Scotch, mineral water, orange juice, and ice. Hosch carried a trayful of glasses.

Löff and the prosecutor went for the orange juice. Everybody else had Scotch and soda.

Soon after drinks were served we heard the jangle of a bunch of keys. All except for Karin Futt held their breath.

"Paul!"

Before I could grab her, she bounced out of her chair and ran to the door.

"Paul, I haven't told them anything! Believe me! Please believe me, I didn't tell them anything—Paul ..."

Futt was about to extricate himself from her embrace when he saw me at the other end of the hall. He froze for a second. Then he pushed his wife to the floor. She curled up next to the wall and bawled. I motioned to him with the Parabellum. Futt put his keys back in his pocket and took out a cigar.

"Come on in. You've kept us all waiting."

He bit the end off the cigar, spat it onto the Persian rug, and swaggered slowly toward me.

"Who's waiting for me?"

"Assorted folks."

As he entered the living room, his eyes widened in horror. Everybody greeted him with a slight nod. Hosch's puzzled expression seemed an indication that he was indeed ready to act the dupe.

"Have a seat, Mr. Futt. Let's get started."

"Started? With what?"

"Just a minute."

I produced Löff's tape recorder and set it on the table. Then I began my lecture.

"On the nineteenth of February nineteen seventy-nine, Vasif Ergün—who was, until his death, a foreign worker in this country—had a traffic accident. He collided with an automobile driven by one Albert Schönbaum. He had not observed the right-of-way ..."

"Excuse me, but what is all this?"

"You know very well what this is, Mr. Futt. Pull yourself together. The jig is up. It won't be all that bad for you. After all, you're a detective superintendent."

I continued. I told them about the deal Vasif Ergün had made with Futt and Eiler, dictated Albert Schönbaum's address to the prosecutor, pointed out existing documents that proved my story, and then proceeded to discuss Ahmed Hamul's entry into the narcotics business. I gave the attorney the names of Hanna Hecht and her friend, as well as that of Mrs. Ergün, described the murder of Vasif Ergün and the farmer's daughter, described the murder weapon, Eiler's nightstick, cited the witnesses Erwin Schöller, Dr. Langner, and the inhabitants of the village on the outskirts of Kronberg, and arrived at the point shortly before Ahmed Hamul's murder. Hosch gave a wonderful performance. Both Futt and Eiler kept glancing at him, visibly perturbed. Hosch groaned, kept saying "oh no, no", ran his hands through his hair, trembled, sucked frantically on his cigarette, and generally mimed a breakdown far better than Eiler had managed to do. When he seemed close to tears as I described the murders, Futt lost his cool.

"Georg! That's enough!"

I had taken care not to bring up Georg Hosch's name until then; I had no doubt that the prosecutor would get around to him soon enough. So far, he had been very busy taking notes.

"And to disperse any doubts that may linger in your mind, I will now let you hear Mr. Eiler voluntarily answering a few questions I put to him."

Eiler attempted to lodge a protest against my wording and pointed at his disfigured face, but after Futt's smile told him that there was nothing he could do to improve his situation, he desisted.

The tape ran, and the case was practically over. Löff and I nodded to each other. Just before the name Hosch was mentioned, I stopped the tape.

"Up to here, everything seems to be taken care of. All that remains is the murder of Ahmed Hamul."

"May I interrupt you for a moment, Mr. Kayankaya? Your story so far does sound plausible. The one thing I don't understand is why we were told there were three suspects here. So far, I only have the names of Futt and Eiler in my notes. May I ask what part Georg Hosch played in this affair?"

"It was he who purloined the heroin from the confiscated supplies at police headquarters. He was able to do that because he was in charge of the monthly burnings of the stuff. But I think it would be best if you asked him yourself."

The prosecutor nodded at Hosch.

"I know that this may strain your credulity, sir, but I am completely stunned by what we have just heard. I don't know what to think anymore. It's all so incredible ... I am absolutely horrified to hear what it seems I must have been involved in ... it is ghastly ..."

"Please express yourself a little more clearly."

"But you see, I didn't know anything about all this ..."

"Stop it, Georg! You're making me sick! Pull yourself together!"

Futt slapped the table top. He had realized that he was a loser, and now he wanted to get the whole thing over with.

"Quiet, please. Mr. Hosch, tell me about it."

He had liked my suggestion about the secret service. He described how four years ago Futt had transferred him to the Narcotics Squad. Soon thereafter Futt had told him about his connections to the Military Intelligence Agency and had explained to him that drugs played a considerable part in the activities of the world's secret intelligence services. It was not, however, in the MIA's interest to let such knowledge become public. Then, Hosch said, Futt had entrusted him with the destruction of confiscated drugs, saying that this put him in a position to assist the intelligence service. And all these years he, Georg Hosch, had purloined heroin from the confiscated stores with a good conscience and in the belief that he was serving the state. After Mr. Futt had become a detective superintendent in charge of criminal cases, it had struck Hosch as a little strange that he was still supposed to keep on delivering the drugs to Futt, but it had, after all, been an assignment given to him by a superior officer, and since it was for the secret service, there was no telling...anything was possible there. He had read in the paper about similar activities involving the American CIA.

"...however, a short while ago Mr. Futt informed me that I could stop deliveries for a while, since they had enough for the time being. I didn't really know what to think about that at all..."

Hosch had stuck to our deal. He even surpassed my expectations.

It was, however, impossible to prevent Futt from bursting into raucous laughter.

"God, Hosch, what a cunning bastard you are! I never knew you were such a great actor."

Perturbed, the prosecutor looked at both of them, then at me. He seemed to have lost the thread of the proceedings.

"Shut your mouth, Futt! Let's get on with Hamul's murder. You'll have plenty of time to laugh later."

Futt resigned himself merely to grinning through all that followed.

Last Friday, on the fifth of August, around six o'clock in the evening, Ahmed Hamul was found murdered in a rear courtyard near the railroad station. The aforementioned Hanna Hecht has testified that Ahmed Hamul wanted out of the drug business. Further proof for that is a house in northern Germany for which he had made a down payment. It was his intention to move there with his family, in order to avoid persecution from his former business partners. Unfortunately, he was prevented from realizing that plan."

Georg Hosch clutched his forehead in a gesture worthy of Duse.

"Oh, now I can see it! Of course. Once Ahmed Hamul was murdered, there could no longer be anyone to sell my heroin consignments!"

I had been keeping an eye on Harry Eiler. When he cried out, jumped up, and rushed at Hosch, I knocked him out for a while.

The prosecutor gasped and rose to his feet.

"I'm sorry, but I had to do it. Please take your seat again. It's taken care of."

"I must say I am not used to behaviour of this sort."

"Me neither, under normal circumstances. Did you get all that down? All you need now is to find out where Harry Eiler was on the fifth of August around six pm. Except for that piece of information, I think you have an open and shut case."

"You're right. Arrest warrants will be issued immediately."

"You may add three cases of grievous bodily harm to the charges."

I handed him Hanna Hecht's blackmail letter."

"'Murderer Futt, get a million and a kilo ready. You'll hear from us soon!' What does that mean?"

"Hanna Hecht, Ahmed Hamul's girlfriend, knew where Ahmed was getting his supplies. After he was killed, she suspected the same murderers we are dealing with here, and tried to collect on that knowledge."

"What about the grievous bodily harm?"

"As soon as I found this note here, in this apartment, I drove over to Hanna Hecht's place. I found Mr. Eiler busy torturing her, and a friend of hers unconscious in the kitchen. You may visit those two in the hospital."

"I must indeed do so. They are important witnesses."

"The third person attacked is myself. My face does not always look like this—you have to take my word for it."

"Yes. And?"

"Futt managed to assign Hamul's murder case to himself and then simply shelved it. But he was not able to prevent Hamul's widow from hiring me as a private investigator. First I received a threatening note in which I was told to leave the case alone, and then on that same evening someone tried to run over me with a Fiat, right in front of my door. Yesterday a masked monster appeared in my office wielding a tear-gas launcher, fired two grenades, and kicked my face in. Make of that what you will."

Hosch thanked me for the (singular) monster with a brief glance.

"May I call my attorney?"

"Certainly, Mr. Futt."

We grinned at each other. Futt did not want to admit defeat, least of all to a Turk. I lit a cigarette and waved my thumb.

"But before you call you lawyer, let's take the prosecutor to the bedroom so you can show him your camping gear."

"I should have pulled your license much sooner."

"And you shouldn't have engaged in such risky business."

The prosecutor tapped me on the shoulder.

"Excuse me, but why do we have to look at his camping gear?"

"It can't hurt."

We went to the bedroom, and Futt emptied out his backpack. The plastic heroin envelopes landed at the prosecutor's feet. He knew immediately what they were, and took them as evidence.

"Can I make my phone all now?"

This time only I grinned.

"Sure, Mr. Futt. In fact, you might first call headquarters and tell them to send a van for the arrest of several drug dealers. I'm sure you know the number."

After Futt had gone to the phone, the prosecutor shook my hand.

"Good work."

"Thank you. Now it's your turn."

"Trust me, I'll take care of it."

While waiting for the police, we busied ourselves protecting Hosch from Harry Eiler, who had regained consciousness, and trying to cajole Mrs. Futt into emerging from her bedroom. She had locked herself in.

Futt sucked pensively on his cigar. I made myself a drink and sat down next to him.

"Was it your idea, that performance of Georg's?"

He didn't look at me, just stared straight ahead.

"Guess so."

"He may get away with it for now. But I'll get his ass in court."

"I know."

"What an idiot he must be, to let you con him into that. I wouldn't have thought he was that dumb."

"Guess he panicked. But it's just fine by me if the two of you tear each other apart in court…Why didn't you just kill me right away?"

"Good question. But your connection to Ahmed Hamul would have been too obvious."

"Yeah, it gets sticky when you have to sweep a murder under the rug, even when you didn't have anything to do with it."

"Uh huh."

The doorbell rang, and a bunch of cops stormed in like a Tartar horde. After the prosecutor had explained to them what was going on, they all suffered a mild identity crisis. They didn't find it easy to arrest Detective Superintendent Futt for dealing heroin, and their colleague Harry for murder. No way, they couldn't just throw their buddies in jail like that. It had to be some kind of mistake. Finally Futt himself had to explain matters and order the arrests. After a few remarks to the effect that they would have preferred to arrest that Turk, the squad left the apartment with the prosecutor and the arrestees and drove off to the jail.

Löff, Katrin Futt, and I stayed behind.

We managed to coax the superintendent's wife out of her room, planted her in front of the television set, placed the bottle of Scotch next to her, and took our leave.

5

Löff and I sat nursing our fourth round of beers. It was a few minutes before six o'clock. The happy hour crowd was congregating at the bar, clamouring for "a schnapps and a beer". Intimacy increased in direct ratio to the number of glasses that slid across the counter. Soni behind the bar had a wide ass, an easy target for male paws. Most of the time she didn't even try to brush them off, her ass was part of her job. Löff's eyelids were drooping, and I began to worry that I would have to give him a ride home.

"Lishen, Kayankaya, you did a goo', a good job, but—"

"—but a good defense attorney can get the charges for Ahmed Hamul's murder dropped. Because there's nothing but circumstantial evidence for it. Right?"

He had already explained that to me five or six times.

"Thash ri'... even though it's quite obvious, only hard evidence is wha' countsh in a trial. Thash right."

"Let's see if Harry Eiler can manufacture an alibi for the fifth of August. They'll throw everything else at him, anyway. Futt and Hosch will take every opportunity to make sure that happens."

"Thash right."

The flesh around my cracked rib was throbbing. I started fantasising about the next three days. Fresh sheets on the bed, a stack of travel and vacation brochures for the morning, various television magazines for the afternoon, then full length movie features in the evening. No quiz or game shows run by idiots, with idiots, and for idiots. The news, then Bogart.

I shook Löff's shoulder. He seemed to be hypnotised by Soni's ass.

"Mr. Löff, I have to get going. I still have to pay my respects to the Ergüns, and tell them what happened, and then I need to hit the sack."

"Right, right...I better get on home too...I think I have a little buzz on."

"And thank you again. I couldn't have done it without your help. I'll drop by your house in a day or two."

"Please do. My old lady will be glad to see you."

I waved to Soni, and she brought the check. I paid. Löff winked at her. We left.

Then, all of a sudden, it was nine thirty. I had walked Loff back to his Mercedes and had gone to my office to pick up the thousand-mark bill. Then home, a shower, bite to eat.

Now I pocketed the change Madame Hulk had given me and the three chocolate bars I had purchased for Ilter Hamul's children. I wished Madame a good evening.

"Same to you."

The sun had set, and except for a couple of pink clouds the sky was empty and blue. Some dark birds were circling high above. I was tired.

Ilter Hamul came to the door. She was wearing a dark green satin robe.

"Good evening. Excuse me for dropping in so late, but I wanted to let you know that the case has been solved. We found the murderer, and he is behind bars."

Her face brightened, she almost smiled. She invited me in and asked me what I would like to drink.

"I wouldn't say no to some coffee."

She ushered me into the large, colourful living room, seated me in an easy chair, and disappeared. Ten minutes later a cup of good strong Turkish coffee stood steaming in front of me.

"This is for your kids."

She thanked me extravagantly for the chocolate and asked me to tell her what had happened. For the second time that day I went over the whole story. I couldn't leave Hanna Hecht out of it, even though I would have liked to spare Ilter's feelings.

She listened in attentive silence, shaking her head now and again. When I had finished, the living room was immersed in darkness. Through the window we could see the moon rise. For a while we sat there in silence, then Ilter Hamul got up and switched on the light. There were tears on her face.

"How can I thank you?"

"Give me change for that bill. At two hundred a day, I get six hundred. That'll do it."

She went to get the money and gave it to me, with a firm handshake.

"Is your brother at home?"

"He's in his room, packing. He is going to Turkey tomorrow."

"I would like to have a word with him."

"Come with me."

She took my arm, and we went to a door that stood ajar. Light shone through the crack onto the floor of the dark hall. Ilter Hamul left me there. I knocked quietly and went in without waiting for a reply. Yilmaz Ergün was bending over a half-packed suitcase. He turned and looked at me over his shoulder. His room contained an unmade bed, an open wardrobe, two chairs, and a nightstand with a radio alarm clock. The only decoration on the wall was a calendar published by the town of Heidelberg.

He straightened his back and turned around, holding three folded shirts.

"Mind if I smoke?"

He nodded reluctantly and dropped the shirts in the suitcase.

"Please, keep on packing, I don't want to interrupt you. Although I want to assure you that there's no need for you to go away."

I lit my cigarette and pulled up a chair. Yilmaz Ergün sat down on the bed.

"Cigarette?"

"No thanks, I don't smoke."

He looked at me with a serious, almost sad expression.

"What did you mean by that—there no need for me to go away?"

I took a couple of puffs on my cigarette.

"What I meant was that no one is looking for you for

the murder of your brother-in-law."

He bent forward and hid his face in his hands. I could only see the shiny black hair on the top of his head. I had time to smoke another couple of cigarettes before he looked up again.

"How did you know..."

"The knife. Only amateurs use a knife. I never made inquiries, but I assume it was a kitchen knife?"

"Yes. It was."

"You never liked Ahmed Hamul, did you? Your father favoured him over you. Vasif always thought you were second-rate. All the approval you got came from your mother."

"Stop!"

"I'm sorry. You probably thought that it was Ahmed Hamul who dragged your father into those drug deals. In actual fact, your father was blackmailed into it. That's how his troubles began. Then, later, he helped Ahmed get into the business. For three years you harboured rage and sorrow over the dissension in your family. It seemed to you that it had to be Ahmed Hamul's fault. When your father died, I'm sure you thought about kicking Ahmed out of the house. But since he hardly came home anymore anyway, and out of kindness to your sister, you didn't do it—your sister Ilter, that is. Because it was what happened to your sister Ayse that finally drove you to kill Ahmed. You couldn't forgive him for getting Ayse hooked on heroin. I think that the day you found out about it was the day when you first thought of killing him. With the passage of time, what had begun as an idea struck you as more and more inevitable. It must have seemed like a solution to all your problems. You would have your revenge for the jealousy of all those years, and your family could live in peace, at long last. Ayse's addiction gave moral justification to the deed. And so, what had been only an idea became a plan, a task. For the salvation of the family."

Yilmaz Ergun sat cowering on his bed, completely motionless. I wasn't sure that he was still listening to me.

"But you are not a gifted murderer, not even as an amateur. You made two stupid mistakes. First of all: no alibi. Ilter told me that you get off work a little before six, and that you are usually home by six o'clock. I have no idea how you got hold of Hanna Hecht's telephone number, but..."

"I tailed him once and read the name on the door. Then I looked it up in the phone book."

"In any case, you called him there on the fifth of August and asked him to meet you somewhere in the neighbourhood. Right after work. If I asked you where exactly you were at that time, you probably couldn't tell me. Isn't that so?"

He nodded.

"The second mistake: if you work in a restaurant kitchen, you don't just grab the first carving knife that comes to hand to kill your brother-in-law with."

I paused for a moment. He still didn't move.

"If someone had decided that you were a suspect, or if the detective who was supposed to investigate the murder hadn't happened to be the murderer of your father—and he'll probably take the rap for Ahmed's murder as well—then you'd be behind bars right now."

He stared at me with wide eyes.

"The murderer of—my father? But—"

"That is another story. Let Ilter tell you about it. I am bushed."

I got up and stood at the door.

"Did you know that Ahmed wanted to get out of the business? When you drove that carving knife into his back, he was about to make a payment on a house in northern Germany. In a couple of months he would have moved there with your family. He had already found a place for Ayse to take the cure. You should have asked him what his plans were. You could have talked with him. And you could have spared yourself from becoming a murderer."

We stared at each other for what seemed an eternity.

"Do you know why I am not handing you over to the cops?"

He shook his head, looking sad.

"Because you will have to deal with what you did for the rest of your life. It doesn't feel good to know you're a murderer, and it feels even worse when the murder was completely pointless. But if it's any consolation to you, I'm the only one who knows."

I tapped the side of my head.

"Good luck, Mr. Ergün. Happy days in Istanbul."

I pulled the door shut quietly and tiptoed down the dark hall and out of the apartment. The staircase was dimly lit and still filled with the heat of the day. I lit a cigarette. As I walked downstairs, the gentle notes of a jazz saxophone wafted out of one of the apartments. I thought about a girl I had known a long time ago.

Then I bought a bottle of Chivas from Madame Hulk and walked home through the night.

JAKOB ARJOUNI'S KAYANKAYA THRILLERS AVAILABLE FROM MELVILLE HOUSE

KISMET

978-1-935554-23-3 | $15.00 US / $17.50 CAN

As a Turkish immigrant raised by Germans, Kemal Kayankaya is regularly subjected to racism in gritty, working-class Frankfurt, and getting work isn't easy. So when his friend Rosario asks him to protect his business against some battle-hardened Croation thugs demanding protection money, the down-and-out Kayankaya takes the job.

HAPPY BIRTHDAY, TURK!

978-1-935554-20-2 | $14.95 US / $16.95 CAN

The police aren't interested when a Turkish immigrant is murdered in the red light district, but wisecracking detective Kayankaya suspects there's something bigger going on, and, unfortunately, he's right....

MORE BEER

978-1-935554-43-1 | $14.95 US / $16.95 CAN

Coming in June 2011

Four eco-terrorists caught vandalizing a chemical plant are also accused of murdering the head of the plant, but witness say there were five men. They hire Kayankaya to help them find the mysterious fifth man.

ONE MAN, ONE MURDER

978-1-935554-54-7 | $14.95 US / $16.95 CAN

Coming in October 2011

When Kayankaya is hired to find a missing young Thai woman, Kayankaya launches a trawl through the immigration offices and brothels of Frankfurt and discovers that lots of young asylum seekers seem to be disappearing into the Frankfurt night.